illustrated by
BRETT HELQUIST

STRANGEVILLE SCHOOL IS TOTALLY NORMAL

by
DARCY MILLER

RANDOM HOUSE 🏠 NEW YORK

Text copyright © 2021 by Darcy Miller
Cover art and interior illustrations copyright © 2021 by Brett Helquist

Visit us on the Web! rhcbooks.com

Educators and librarians, for a variety of teaching tools,
visit us at RHTeachersLibrarians.com

Library of Congress Cataloging-in-Publication Data
Names: Miller, Darcy, author. | Helquist, Brett, illustrator.
Title: Strangeville School is totally normal / Darcy Miller ;
[illustrated by] Brett Helquist.
Description: First edition. | New York : Random House Children's Books,
2021. | Series: Strangeville School ; 1 | Audience: Ages 8–12. | Summary:
"Harvey Hill's first day at Strangeville Middle School doesn't go quite as
expected when he discovers it's full of various creatures and odd happenings,
including a particularly nefarious supply closet"—Provided by publisher.
Identifiers: LCCN 2021008580 (print) | LCCN 2021008581 (ebook) |
ISBN 978-0-593-30950-6 (trade) | ISBN 978-0-593-30961-2 (lib. bdg.) |
ISBN 978-0-593-30962-9 (ebook)
Subjects: LCSH: Middle schools—Juvenile fiction. | Missing persons—
Juvenile fiction. | Monsters—Juvenile fiction. | Horror tales. | Humorous
stories. | CYAC: Middle schools—Fiction. | Schools—Fiction. | Missing
persons—Fiction. | Monsters—Fiction. | Horror stories. | Humorous
stories. | LCGFT: Horror fiction. | Humorous fiction.
Classification: LCC PZ7.1.M565 St 2021 (print) |
LCC PZ7.1.M565 (ebook) | DDC 813.6 [Fic]—dc23

The artist used oil on paper to create the illustrations for this book.
The text of this book is set in 11.65-point
New Century Schoolbook LT Pro.
Interior design by Jen Valero

Printed in the United States of America
10 9 8 7 6 5 4 3 2 1
First Edition

For all the weirdos out there.
But especially Ben. —DM

For Colleen, my mother. —BH

Contents

1

Morning Announcements

Good morning, Strangeville School! This is Vice Principal Capozzi, filling in for Principal Gupta, who you'll be happy to hear is recovering nicely from her unfortunate piranha incident yesterday.

I've been assured by Janitor Gary that all carnivorous fish have now been removed from the first-floor drinking fountains. So if you happen to see Janitor Gary today, make sure to give him a big Strangeville thank-you!

In related news, Nurse Porter informs me that we are temporarily out of Band-Aids. In the event of a paper cut, Nurse Porter recommends "having known better than to handle paper in the first place" and "honestly, you probably deserved it."

Well said, Nurse Porter. Strangeville is lucky to have you!

Moving right along to the lunch menu, it looks as though today's choices will include steamed Maine lobster on watercress; unseasoned, lukewarm gruel; and, oh! A special new menu item! Chef Louis is describing it as "complete and total darkness, but in meat loaf form."

Mmm, mmm. Sounds delicious, Chef Louis!

On a more serious note, I'd like to remind all students to try to avoid angering the third-floor supply closet today. In fact, why not avoid the third floor altogether? I know I will!

And, finally, I'd like to welcome new student Harvey Hill to Strangeville School this morning. Harvey hails from back east and will be joining Mr. Sandringham's fifth-grade homeroom. I'm told he has "brownish hair," "average elbows," and "definitely a nose of some sort." So if you see anyone matching that description today, wish them hello!

This is Vice Principal Capozzi, signing off. Have a fantastic day, Strangeville School! But not *too* fantastic. You know the supply closet doesn't like that. . . .

Harvey

In Mr. Sandringham's fifth-grade homeroom, twenty-two sets of eyes turned in Harvey Hill's direction.

Well, twenty-*three* sets of eyes, if you counted the classroom lizard, Mr. Pickles.

Harvey, who had not yet noticed Mr. Pickles and was, therefore, unaware of the lizard's existence, did not.

It was fine.

Mr. Pickles was used to being overlooked.

One day, the lizard often thought, he would have his revenge. Mr. Pickles had plans. Oh yes,

Mr. Pickles had *big* plans. *Terrifying* plans. Plans that would make you shoot up in bed in the middle of the night, sweating from head to toe, if you knew them. Plans so dastardly evil, so *incomprehensibly fiendish,* that to even understand the smallest part of them would make your teeth chatter and your bones rattle and your very *soul* quiver in its boots.

But, anyway.

Enough about Mr. Pickles!

Let's get back to Harvey.

"Would you like to come up and introduce yourself, Harvey?" Mr. Sandringham asked. He squinted thoughtfully at the new student's elbows. It was difficult to see from the front of the classroom, but they *appeared* to be average. Then again, elbows were a tricky thing. Mr. Sandringham had been fooled by elbows before.

"Um . . . okay," Harvey said, a touch of reluctance in his voice. Strangeville may have been his fourth new school in as many years, but introducing himself in front of the class never got any easier. He pushed himself out of his chair and made his way to the front of the room, feeling the weight of twenty-two pairs of eyes following each step (twenty-*three,* counting Mr. Pickles, of course).

"So, um, hi," Harvey said, giving an uncertain wave. Harvey was tall for his age, with wavy brown hair, thirty-seven freckles, and a mysterious secret. "My name's Harvey Hill. Which, I guess, you already knew." He swallowed nervously, tugging at the bottom of his shirt. "My family just moved here from Boston, and, er . . . I like video games, and taking pictures, and . . . um . . . yeah. I guess that's it?" he finished hopefully.

"Wonderful," Mr. Sandringham said, beaming in approval. "I know we're all hoping Strangeville will finally be a fit for you, Harvey! How are you liking it so far?"

Harvey shifted from one foot to the other. "Um, it seems . . . good? I liked the morning announcements. They were funny."

Mr. Sandringham's forehead wrinkled in confusion. "Funny?"

"Yeah. You know, all that stuff about the piranhas, and the lunch menu, and the supply closet?" Harvey asked. "At my other schools, they never joked around in the morning announcements."

Mr. Sandringham's face paled.

The classroom grew still.

Even Mr. Pickles looked alarmed.

"I assure you," Mr. Sandringham told Harvey, nervously twisting his necktie, "there is nothing *funny* about the supply closet."

Harvey blinked.

The teacher straightened his shoulders, visibly composing himself. "Don't worry," he said. "You'll learn all about Strangeville soon enough. I've asked one of your classmates, Stella Cho, to show you around the school today. Stella, could you raise your hand?"

He peered expectantly around the room, but no hands appeared in the air.

"Oh dear," Mr. Sandringham said. "Stella seems to be missing." He clicked his tongue in annoyance. "Oh well, I'm sure she'll turn up at some point. Students usually do! In the meantime, before the bell rings for first period, does anyone have any questions for Harvey?"

Twenty-two hands shot upward.

"Do you know where I left my hockey pads?"

"How do you calculate the square root of ninety-one?"

"What's the fastest way to get to Toledo, Ohio?"

"Why do your own farts smell good, but everyone else's smell bad?"

"What's the meaning of life, anyway?"

"Excellent questions, everyone," Mr. Sandringham said, beaming at his class. He turned to look at the new student. "Harvey?"

Harvey blinked again, taking a half step backward.

Twenty-two pairs of eyes (Mr. Pickles had fallen asleep by this point) peered up at him, waiting for his response.

"Um . . . ," Harvey said, "could I have the bathroom pass, please?"

The Bathroom Pass

H arvey stepped into the hallway, cradling the bathroom pass carefully in his arms.

At Harvey's last school, the bathroom pass had been a small, laminated piece of paper with the words BATHROOM PASS written across the front.

At Strangeville, the bathroom pass was a gold-fish bowl.

With every step, the water in the bowl sloshed back and forth, threatening to spill over the edges. Inside, a single goldfish swam in lazy circles, look-ing unimpressed.

The goldfish's name was Brad.

(Don't get too attached to Brad, by the way; he dies in chapter 18.)

Walking slowly, Harvey set off down the hall, searching for the nearest bathroom. Rows of lockers lined the walls, hung with brightly colored posters:

VOTE FLARSKY FOR CLASS PRESIDENT!

CHESS CLUB TRYOUTS THIS WEEK!

REMEMBER, THE SUPPLY CLOSET IS ALWAYS WATCHING!

Harvey paused in front of the last sign, reading it several times.

He was just about to move on when the nearest classroom door flew open, making him jump. Water slopped down the front of his T-shirt, surprisingly cold and smelling slightly of Brad.

A girl poked her head out of the doorway, frowning at Harvey. She was short for her age, with a long black ponytail, thirty-*eight* freckles, and a highly developed sense of curiosity. "Are you here from the agency?"

"Um," Harvey said. "I—"

"Never mind," the girl interrupted, shaking her head. "You're late!"

"Er . . ." Harvey glanced down at the goldfish bowl in his arms. "Actually, I was just . . . looking for the bathroom?"

"There's no time for that now," the girl said impatiently. "You'll have to wait!" She reached out and hauled Harvey into the classroom, the goldfish bowl tilting dangerously to one side.

"I think there's been a mistake," Harvey said, stumbling through the doorway and into the empty science classroom behind her. "I'm—"

"Here about the rat problem," the girl interrupted, finishing his sentence for him. "I know, I'm the one who called *you,* remember? Stella Cho," she said, sticking out her hand. "Lead reporter for the *Strangeville School Gazette.* Also, fifth-grade student."

"Oh," Harvey said, recognizing the name. Balancing the goldfish bowl in the crook of his arm, he reached out to awkwardly shake her hand. "Hi. Actually, I think you're supposed to be showing me—"

"Where Cuddles is," Stella said, interrupting him again. "What do you think I'm trying to do? Anyway, I'm pretty sure he's somewhere in the ventilation system." She pointed at the open air-vent cover in the corner. A stepladder stood ready underneath.

Harvey peered up at the ceiling in alarm. "Cuddles?" he asked.

Stella sighed in exasperation. "The class rat!" She took the goldfish bowl from him and set it down on the nearest desk. "It's my turn to feed him this week, but when I came in this morning, his cage was empty. He must have escaped. Just look what he did to everyone's science-fair projects!"

She gestured toward the counter at the back of the room, which was lined with a display of brightly colored poster boards. The projects in front were in various states of disarray: baking-soda volcanoes tipped on their sides, oozing puddles of lava, and plastic petri dishes pushed to the floor, their contents spilling haphazardly onto the carpet. There were broken bottles and toppled models and a partially eaten diorama of the rain forest ecosystem.

"Oh," Harvey said. "Right. Um, the thing is, I'm

not really . . . I mean . . . maybe you should ask your teacher for help?" he finished hopefully.

"I'd love to," Stella said. "Only Ms. Crumbleton disappeared last week."

"What do you mean, 'disappeared'?" Harvey asked.

"Vanished? Vamoosed? Went missing?" Stella paused. "You know, *disappeared*." She shook her head disapprovingly. "According to the rumors, she left to get a new pen and never came back."

"Oh," Harvey said again. He reached up, clutching reassuringly at the straps of his backpack. "Well . . . Don't get me wrong, I'd love to help, but—"

"Excellent," Stella interrupted, giving a brisk nod of approval. "Let's get going, then."

And, before Harvey quite knew what was happening, he found himself blinking down at Stella from the inside of the air shaft. "Are you sure about this?" he asked.

"You'll be fine," Stella said, handing him a flashlight. "Just remember what I told you about Cuddles on the phone: there's a *slight* chance he might have ingested some of the serum from Nevaeh's science-fair project, so whatever you do, do *not,* under *any* circumstances—"

Brrrrriiiiiinnnggg!

The first-period bell rang, cutting her off.

"Oops!" Stella said, clattering down the ladder. "Got to run!"

"Wait," Harvey called after her, panicking slightly. "Under any circumstances don't do *what?*"

"I'll check back after music class!" Stella called, ducking out the classroom door. "Good luck!"

Harvey stared after her, the flashlight clenched tightly in his fist. From the air shaft behind him came a loud and ominous *thump.*

"Well," Harvey said aloud to the empty room. "That can't be good."

Cuddles

Okay, Harvey thought, inching forward on his stomach through the pitch-black ventilation shaft. *Nothing to worry about. This is fine. This is all totally fine.*

Another loud thump echoed through the air shaft. Harvey swept his flashlight back and forth in front of him, trying not to panic.

"Cuddles?" Harvey called out. "Is that you?"

His words echoed forlornly down the shaft, disappearing into the darkness ahead of him.

There was no reply.

Of course there's no reply, Harvey told himself,

crawling forward on his (utterly run-of-the-mill) elbows. *He's a rat. Rats don't talk.*

There was another thump, followed this time by an even more ominous scratching sound. It was like the scrape of twenty sharp little claws against a metal floor.

Only, for some reason, the claws didn't sound so little.

"Cuddles?" Harvey called, snapping his fingers together hopefully. "Here, Cuddles! Be a good rat!"

His backpack bumping against the top of the vent, he pushed his way forward another few feet, coming to a T in the ventilation shaft. Either way he looked, the air shaft seemed to stretch into oblivion, the light from his flashlight fading away into darkness.

"Well, now what?" Harvey asked himself, peering back and forth down the tunnel.

From the right side of the tunnel came another thump, even louder than before.

Thump!

Scrape!

Thump!

Scrape!

"Cuddles?" Harvey whispered.

In the weak beam of his flashlight, two flashes of red suddenly appeared. An enormous rat emerged from the darkness, its huge, pointed teeth bared in a snarl and its strange, ruby-colored eyes glowing like fire.

It was the size of a golden retriever.

Harvey swallowed, wondering what sort of

science-fair project Nevaeh had been working on. He wished he could reach his camera, but he'd tucked it away in his backpack for safekeeping earlier that morning.

In front of him, Cuddles let out a growl.

"Good Cuddles," Harvey said faintly. He hadn't even known that rats *could* growl until that very moment.

Cuddles growled again.

Feeling in his shirt pocket, Harvey pulled out the Reese's peanut-butter cup that he had been saving for a midmorning snack. It was slightly squashed from his recent travels through the air vent, but still good.

"Mmm." Harvey shook the peanut-butter cup enticingly in the giant rat's direction. "Yummy."

Cuddles lifted his chin, sniffing the air with his grotesquely whiskered snout.

"Cuddles want a treat?" Harvey asked hopefully. He tossed the peanut-butter cup in the giant rat's direction, watching as the candy skidded across the metal floor and landed next to Cuddles's massive, gnarled feet.

Cuddles lowered his head, sniffing the peanut-butter cup suspiciously.

"Go on, Cuddles," Harvey urged. "Yum!"

In one swift movement, the giant rat snatched the still-wrapped candy from the floor, swallowing it whole.

Harvey abruptly realized that he didn't have a follow-up plan. He was trapped in a ventilation shaft with an enormous mutant rat.

An enormous, *hungry* mutant rat.

An enormous, hungry mutant rat *whose appetite he had just whetted.*

There was a brief pause.

Harvey stared at Cuddles.

Cuddles stared at Harvey.

In the classroom below, Brad the goldfish swam in slow, lazy laps, unaware of the epic stare-down taking place above his head.

Not that Brad would have cared about an epic stare-down.

Brad's entire life was an epic stare-down. Goldfish don't have eyelids; he literally *couldn't* blink, even if he wanted to.

Goldfish are also missing stomachs, which makes them hypersensitive to overfeeding. Their average life span is five to ten years, although the oldest goldfish on record lived for over forty years. In later life, Tish the goldfish faded from bright orange to a distinguished silver, but he remained healthy until shortly before his death. Upon his passing, he was buried in a yogurt container in his owners' garden.

But, anyway.

Enough about goldfish!

Let's get back to Harvey.

With every passing second, Cuddles was growing larger in front of his eyes.

It was as if an invisible mouth was inflating a large, rat-shaped balloon: with every puff, Cuddles expanded outward.

His enormous feet doubled in size, gigantic claws digging into the metal air shaft like nails on a blackboard. His snout lengthened and stretched; his red eyes bulged like baseballs. His body seemed to swell, his sides and back pressing against the walls of the ventilation system, straining against the metallic confines like an overripe watermelon about to burst.

The air shaft gave an ominous creak.

The floor beneath Harvey began to tilt.

The rat continued to grow—bigger, and bigger, and *bigger*—until finally, with an earsplitting shriek of protesting metal, the air shaft gave out beneath his bulk.

As Harvey watched in disbelief, Cuddles plummeted through the floor in front of him, disappearing in a cloud of dust and broken plaster.

Harvey blinked.

"Well," he said. "That was unexpected."

Curiosity got the best of him. Edging forward on his (perfectly regular) elbows, Harvey peered cautiously over the side of the hole.

In the classroom below, Harvey's new classmates stared up at him in surprise. Clouds of dust drifted down from the ruined ceiling, coating the room in a fine layer of grime.

In the center of the room, Cuddles stood up, shaking dust from his fur.

The rat was now the size of a large pony.

As everyone watched, Cuddles ambled slowly out the door, his massive body barely clearing the frame.

In her chair on the back riser, Stella lowered her instrument to her lap. Her ponytail swung back and forth as she tipped her head up to peer at Harvey, her expression curious.

"Er, sorry about that," Harvey said. He shifted uncomfortably on his (completely mediocre) elbows. There was a long pause as everyone looked around the rubble-strewn classroom.

"So," Harvey asked Stella brightly, changing the subject, "is that a flugelhorn?"

"I really am sorry," Harvey told Stella. He hooked his hands through the straps of his backpack, giving a helpless shrug. "I tried to tell you I wasn't from the agency."

Stella tipped her flugelhorn upside down, watching as a fine stream of dust poured to the floor.

Harvey tugged uncomfortably at his earlobe. "Um . . . should I go find a broom?" he asked, looking toward the teacher.

At the front of the classroom, Ms. Wickham, the music teacher, gave herself a firm shake. Yes, watching a two-hundred-pound rat crash

5

Flugelhorns

T he flugelhorn, as everyone knows, is a bra§
instrument that resembles a cornet but wit
a wider, more conical bore. Invented in Au
tria in the 1830s, it is not to be confused with oth
strangely named musical instruments such as t]
octobass, the didgeridoo, the Sharpsichord, and t]
Majestic Bellowphone.

But, anyway.

Enough about flugelhorns!

Let's get back to Harvey.

He stepped off the ladder Stella had fetch
from the classroom next door, climbing awkwar(
over a twisted section of fallen ductwork.

through the ceiling had been unexpected, but one had to take these things in stride.

"Don't be silly," Ms. Wickham told Harvey. "A little dust never hurt anybody."

"Actually," said one of the flute players, raising her hand, "I'm allergic to dust."

"Me too," said a trombonist. Harvey thought she might be the girl who had asked him about her hockey pads. "Also tree nuts, soy, and the color lavender."

"I'm allergic to kumquats!" called one of the tuba players.

"I'm allergic to robots!" said the other.

"I'm allergic to people named Steven!" said a girl holding a saxophone. She narrowed her eyes in Harvey's direction. "Your name isn't Steven, is it?"

"No," Harvey said, taken aback. "It's Harvey. Remember? From homeroom, a few minutes ago?"

"If you say so," the girl said. She lowered her gaze, peering suspiciously at his (undeniably boring) elbows.

Harvey was beginning to regret choosing a short-sleeved shirt that morning.

"Are you *sure* your name isn't Steven?" The girl, whose name was Nevaeh Taylor, looked down, examining her forearm closely. "Because it feels like I'm starting to get a rash."

The girl next to her drew back in horror, clutching her oboe to her chest. "I'm allergic to rashes!"

"*Everyone*'s allergic to rashes," said the clarinet player.

"I'm allergic to hydraulic chain saws," said the timpani player. "Also shrimp. You don't have any shrimp on you, do you?" he asked Harvey.

"Um . . ." Harvey patted his pockets. "I don't think so?"

"All right, all right," Ms. Wickham said, raising her hands in the air and making a shushing motion. "That's enough, everybody. Harvey, it's wonderful to meet you," she said. "Since it's your first day, why don't you take a seat, and we'll show you what we've been working on?" Ms. Wickham told him. "It's a forty-minute-long experimental jazz composition entitled 'Ode to a Slug'!"

Harvey blinked. "Great," he said weakly.

Stella patted the empty chair next to her. "Here, you can sit next to me," she said. "I have a solo."

"Actually," Harvey admitted, tugging awkwardly at his earlobe again, "I'm allergic to flugelhorns."

Stella

Forty-two minutes later, Harvey stepped into the hallway, rubbing his aching eardrums.

Harvey had never given much thought to slugs before, but now he was *pretty* sure he hated them.

As more classroom doors opened, spilling students into the hallway, Harvey found himself being jostled back and forth in the crowd. He tucked his (utterly unexceptional) elbows close to his body, trying not to be noticed. Even though he was literally surrounded by people, he had never felt more alone.

Harvey wished he was the sort of boy who made friends easily. The sort of boy who knew what to say, or when to laugh, or how to wear his hair.

The sort of boy who *wasn't* harboring a dark, mysterious secret.

The sort of boy who was just, well . . . a *boy*.

The crowd ahead of him parted just long enough for Harvey to glimpse the end of a long pink tail disappearing around the corner.

Cuddles.

Harvey shuddered, feeling a sudden pang of longing for his last school: he hadn't fit in there, either, but at least he hadn't had to worry about giant mutant rats roaming the hallway.

Shaking his head, he shrugged off his backpack and unzipped the main compartment, searching for his new class schedule. He was still rummaging through the folders inside when he ran smack into the shoulder of a familiar black-haired girl.

Both their backpacks fell to the floor, their contents spilling everywhere.

"There you are! Why did you run out of music so fast?" Stella asked Harvey. "I'm supposed to be showing you around, remember?"

He dropped to his knees, anxiously reaching for the camera that had fallen partially out of his bag. An old-fashioned, boxy Canon AE-1, it was Harvey's most treasured possession.

Harvey turned the large black camera back and forth, checking to make sure nothing was broken. To his relief, it looked fine. "Er, sorry," he told Stella, looping the worn red-and-green-striped camera strap over his head. The weight of it around his neck was reassuring. "Here, let me help you," he added, grabbing for a glittery plastic yo-yo that was threatening to roll away. He handed it to Stella and started scooping up the rest of her scattered belongings.

Soon he had amassed a small pile in front of him, including one tube of lip balm, nine pencils, two packs of gum, a library

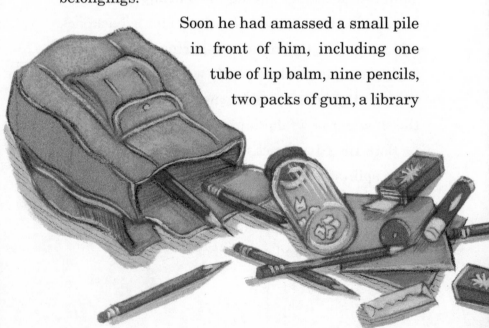

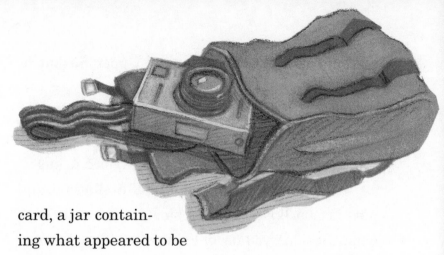

card, a jar contain-
ing what appeared to be
baby teeth, and a small brass token the size of a
nickel.

Harvey held up the jar containing what appeared to be baby teeth. "Are these what they look
like?" he asked.

"I don't trust the Tooth Fairy," Stella said coolly,
taking the jar from him.

"Oh," Harvey said.

As Stella gathered the rest of her things, Harvey
picked up the small metal token, which was stamped
on both sides with an image of a typewriter.

"It's from the Typewriter Museum of Upper Saskatchewan," Stella explained as Harvey turned the
token back and forth, examining it more
closely.

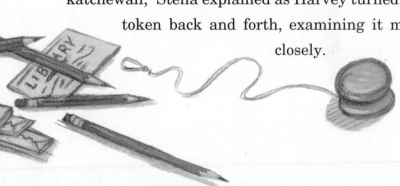

"The Typewriter Museum of Upper Saskatchewan?" Harvey repeated.

"Trust me," Stella said. "It's *way* better than the Typewriter Museum of *Lower* Saskatchewan."

Harvey blinked. "Right," he said. "Good to know."

"You can keep that, if you want," Stella said, zipping her backpack. "I have plenty more of them at home. Besides, you never know when it might come in handy."

"Oh. Er . . . thanks?" Harvey said, not wanting to appear rude. He slipped the token into his pocket.

Stella stood up. "Come on," she said. "We have gym next."

Harvey followed Stella as she strode purposefully down the hallway, her ponytail bouncing with each step. "Cool camera," she offered as they maneuvered through the crowd. "I've never seen one like that before."

"Thanks. It was my grandpa's," Harvey said. "He was a photographer for *National Geographic*. He used to travel all over the world, taking pictures. He even climbed Mount Everest once."

Stella looked impressed.

"Wow," she said. "My grandpa worked for a company that made electric nose-hair trimmers. He used to give me one for my birthday every year."

"Oh," Harvey said. "That's . . . cool too."

It was suddenly very difficult not to stare at Stella's nostrils.

"So, hey, I think I saw Cuddles again, a second ago," he said, changing the subject. Ruefully, he looked down at the camera around his neck. "I wish I could have gotten a picture of him. No one's going to believe me otherwise."

Stella wrinkled her nose. "I should probably call animal control back," she said. "Although I have to admit, I'm curious to see how big he'll get."

Harvey stared at her in alarm. "You mean he's going to get *bigger*?"

"I'm not sure," Stella said thoughtfully. "I'm guessing it depends on how much of the growth serum he ate."

"Growth serum?" Harvey asked blankly.

"Nevaeh's science-fair project," Stella explained. She stopped just outside the gym door, pulling a small notebook from her back pocket and flipping through the pages. "Here it is," she told Harvey, finding her notes for the science-fair article. "Nevaeh

Taylor, 'Biosynthesizing Algae Phytohormones: Grow Bigger Tomatoes in Just Eighty-Seven Easy Steps!'"

Harvey blinked again. "For my last science-fair project, I made a kazoo."

Pulling a freshly sharpened pencil from behind her right ear, Stella flipped to an empty page. "Interesting," she said, scribbling a note down on the paper. "Tell me, is Harvey short for something? Harvander? Harvilliam? Harvgomery?"

"Er, no," Harvey said. "It's just Harvey. Harvey Hill."

Stella raised her eyebrows. "If you say so," she said. "And your family just moved here from Antarctica?"

"Boston," Harvey corrected her. "Boston, Massachusetts."

"Boston?" Stella asked, the tip of her pencil hovering over her notebook. "Are you sure?"

"Of *course* I'm sure," Harvey said. "Why?"

"No reason," Stella said quickly, scribbling another note down on the page. "Is that your real hair color, by the way?"

"Er . . . yes?"

Stella, looking dubious, scribbled another note down on the paper.

"Wait, what are you writing?" Harvey asked. He leaned forward, trying to read Stella's handwriting.

"Nothing," Stella said. She licked the tip of her pencil. "So, Harvey Hill from Boston, Massachusetts. Tell me, what's your secret?"

Harvey's ears went very hot, then very cold.

His hands grew clammy, and his mouth went dry.

His (absolutely average) elbows gave a nervous twitch.

"Secret?" he asked, a little too loudly. "What secret? I don't have a secret!"

Stella gave him a knowing look.

"This is Strangeville," she said. "*Everyone* has a secret." She flipped her notebook shut, shoved it back into her pocket, and reached for the door. "Come on," she told Harvey. "It's time for class."

As she pulled open the door to the gym, an enormous cannonball soared past their shoulders, smashing into the wall behind them.

"Oh, look," Stella said brightly. "It's dodgeball!"

7

Dodgeball

"Now, the rules of dodgeball are simple," Coach Johnson said, planting her fists on her hips. "If you see a ball, dodge it. Any questions?"

Harvey swallowed nervously, raising his hand.

"You there, new kid," Coach Johnson said, pointing at Harvey. "With the elbows."

Harvey swallowed again. "Harvey. Harvey Hill. I guess I'm just wondering . . . we're not actually playing with *all* of these balls, are we?" He gestured toward the row of balls lined up in the center of the gym. Just from where he was standing, Harvey could see a beach ball, a volleyball, a golf ball, a croquet ball, a tetherball, a water-polo ball, and a kloot.

A kloot, of course, is a wooden ball filled with lead, approximately seven centimeters in diameter. It's used in Klootschieten, a popular sport in the Netherlands and parts of Germany, in which participants attempt to throw the kloot as far as they can. The first competitive Klootschieten league was developed in 1902 by Hinrich Dunkhase, who was chairman of the league until his death in 1905.

But, anyway.

Enough about Klootschieten!

Let's get back to Harvey.

"I mean," Harvey continued, pointing at the ball at the end, "you don't really expect us to hit each other with *bowling* balls, do you?"

"Of course not," Coach Johnson barked. "I expect you to *dodge* bowling balls. On my whistle. One, two . . ."

As the shrill blast of the whistle echoed through the gym, Harvey's classmates gave a cheer, surging forward in a frenzied rush for the line of balls.

Harvey ran in the opposite direction, ducking low and hunching protectively over his camera.

A thirty-pound medicine ball flew past, narrowly missing him before smashing into the display case at the far end of the gym.

The glass case shattered, the trophies inside falling like bowling pins.

"Nice shot, Narula!" Coach Johnson shouted in approval. "Way to get in the game!"

Harvey gave a yelp of fear, switching directions.

From the other side of the gym, Nevaeh Taylor yelled, "Fore!" A second later, a golf ball swished past Harvey's head, swooping through the air in a graceful arc before smacking into a dark-haired boy's back. The boy, whose name was Nicolas Flarsky, pitched forward, tripping over his own feet and hitting the floor with a solid *whoomph*.

"Well done, Taylor," Coach Johnson called. "That's a birdie!"

Harvey switched directions again, veering wildly, his heart pounding in his chest. To his left, a girl named Evie Anderson was wrestling with an enormous ball

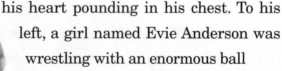

of twine almost
as large as
she was.
A blond
boy next to
her staggered
beneath the weight
of a bowling ball,
attempting to lift
it over his head.

Someone
unleashed a
handful of
gumballs
on the floor,
sending the
small,

brightly colored circles rolling everywhere. Harvey careened to the side, his arms pumping back and forth and his sneakers squeaking on the floor.

"Look alive, new kid!" Coach Johnson yelled. "Let's see some hustle!"

Harvey gave another yelp, ducking low beneath the Wiffle ball that Arjun Narula had just hurled at his face. From the far side of the gym came another crash; Harvey raised his camera, managing to snap a picture as the jagged pieces of the basketball-hoop backboard plummeted to the floor.

It would be a great action shot . . . if Harvey could stay alive long enough to develop the film.

The picked-off students were beginning to make their way to the bleachers, dazed and limping.

Harvey spun around in a circle, his camera clutched to his chest, trying not to panic. Threats loomed from every direction; as Harvey watched, Stella scooped a softball from the floor, winging it gleefully at his nose.

He dropped to the floor, curling his body protectively around his camera.

Surely the game would end soon, he told himself.

"Up and at 'em!" Coach Johnson called, blowing a short blast on her whistle. "No napping on the court!"

Harvey groaned, pushing himself to his feet.

He thought longingly of being trapped in an air shaft with a two-hundred-pound rat.

An enormous beach ball soared through the air in front of him, and Harvey found himself automatically reaching for it, his arms barely wide enough to span the sides.

"Nice work!" Coach Johnson yelled in approval. "You're out, Flarsky!"

Nicolas trotted sulkily toward the bleachers, leaving Harvey surrounded by the rest of the players.

He whirled back and forth in a circle, searching for a way to escape, but he was surrounded on every side, a virtual wall of dodgeballs in every size, shape, and weight.

Harvey heaved the beach ball with everything he had, aiming for the nearest person. The gigantic ball floated through the air, dropping uselessly to the floor a few yards in front of him.

Well, Harvey thought. *So much for that.*

Hunching low over his camera, he closed his eyes tight, waiting for the onslaught to begin.

The sound of Coach Johnson's whistle blasted through the gym. The high-pitched shriek was the sweetest noise Harvey had ever heard in his life.

"That's time!" Coach Johnson shouted. "Rack 'em and stack 'em, people!"

Stella wandered past Harvey, a cannonball tucked beneath her arm. "Fun, right?" she asked.

"So fun," Harvey said weakly.

And then, with a feeble grin, he collapsed to the floor.

8

An Announcement

Good morning again, Strangeville School! Vice Principal Capozzi here, with a quick third-period update regarding the first-floor drinking fountains.

I've just learned that in order to take care of our pesky piranha problem, Janitor Gary may or may not have released a *small* number of baby crocodiles into the water pipes.

Bonus points for creative problem solving, Janitor Gary!

I'm assured these crocodiles pose absolutely *no risk* to humans. Unless, of course, you happen to come into contact with one of them, in which case Janitor Gary informs me you'll "definitely suffer a variety of horrifying injuries, each more gruesome than the last."

Well.

Janitor Gary certainly has a way with words, doesn't he, folks?

On another, more serious note, I'm afraid there have been certain rumblings from the third floor. Rumors that the supply closet is . . . *displeased* have been circulating.

And we all know what happens when the supply closet is displeased. . . .

[throat clearing noises]

Several more substitute teachers have disappeared, leaving behind the scent of burning pencil erasers in their wake, and quiet screams have been heard echoing through the water pipes.

An emergency basket of office supplies, including Post-it notes, sharpened number-two pencils, and dry-erase markers, has been left in the hallway as a sign of goodwill.

Our only option now is to wait, hoping against hope that our efforts to appease the closet have been successful.

In the meantime, I ask you all to remember our

Strangeville School motto: "Be kind. Be safe. Be curious. But most of all, be afraid."

And speaking of fear, it's time for our daily dose of nightmares!

A quick reminder that, per school policy, all students *must* register any nightmares at the front office immediately upon entering the building. After all, the supply closet can't haunt our every waking hour if it doesn't know what we fear, all alone, in the dark of night!

Today's first nightmare comes from sixth grader DeMarius King and reads, "Last night I dreamed that a giant sandwich was chasing me. It would have been fine, but the sandwich was tuna, and I don't like tuna. Next time, I hope I dream about a giant ham-and-cheese sandwich chasing me."

Don't we all, DeMarius. Don't we all!

Next up is seventh grader McKenzie Brian, who writes, "My dream was that I had hot dogs instead of fingers. It was gross."

Thanks for sharing, McKenzie! It certainly *sounds* gross, indeed.

Finally, we have fifth grader Nicolas Flarsky, who writes, "You know that dream where there's a big test at school, and you suddenly realize you haven't studied for it? My dream was like that, only instead of a big test, it was a dolphin. And instead of studying, it was playing golf in the 1996 PGA Championship tournament. Also, my grandma Shirley was there, dressed in a rented bear costume. She kept booing me. Then a real bear attacked me, and I woke up."

Ah yes! I think we've all had *that* dream before, Nicolas!

Well done, Strangeville! Let's keep those nightmares coming. Watch a scary movie before bed tonight! Go for a walk in a cemetery! Read your favorite ghost story! Be creative! But not *too* creative—you know how the supply closet feels about *that*.

This is Vice Principal Capozzi, signing off for now!

Good luck, Strangeville School.

Good luck.

A Small Number of Baby Crocodiles

With the vice principal's ominous warning still ringing in his ears, Harvey heaved the final bowling ball onto the shelf of the gym's equipment cupboard and wiped the sweat from the palms of his hands. His heart was pounding with adrenaline, his legs slightly shaky beneath him.

"We don't play dodgeball *every* day, do we?" he asked Stella, who had just finished wrestling the giant ball of twine into the corner.

"Of course not," Stella said. "Sometimes we play musical chairs."

Harvey felt a swell of relief.

"Although it tends to get a bit violent," Stella said blithely. She gave a final shove to the ball of twine, then turned, looking Harvey critically up and down. "You might want to get a helmet."

"I'll take that under advisement," Harvey said faintly.

Stella tilted her head to the side, still peering at Harvey. "Are you okay?" she asked. "You look a little . . . green."

"I'm fine," Harvey said, swallowing thickly. "I guess I'm just not used to people using my head for shot-put practice. At my last school, we mainly just ran laps in gym. Although we were just about to start our square-dancing unit."

Stella shivered. "That sounds terrifying. Anyway, come on; we have math next."

Harvey followed Stella out of the gym, hurrying to keep pace with her. "So, what's up with the announcements, anyway?" he asked. "I know Mr. Sandringham said they weren't a joke, but are you guys, like, practicing for a school play or something? Or is it some kind of . . . performance art?"

"Performance art?" Stella repeated quizzically.

"Well, I mean, they're obviously not *real*, right?" Harvey asked.

Stella stopped abruptly in the middle of the hallway, turning to look at him.

Harvey tripped over his feet, just barely managing to stop himself from running into her.

"What do you mean?" Stella asked.

Harvey blinked. "Well, you know, like . . . the janitor didn't *really* let a bunch of crocodiles loose in the halls, right?"

"Of course he didn't," Stella said crisply.

Harvey, who hadn't quite realized he was holding his breath, let out a sigh of relief.

He felt a little foolish. *Of course* the announcements weren't real.

"Weren't you listening?" Stella continued. "Janitor Gary released the crocodiles in the *water pipes,* not the halls."

Harvey stared at her. "Wait. Are you telling me that it's not made up? That all that stuff about the supply closet is—"

"True?" Stella finished. "Obviously."

"But that's impossible," Harvey protested.

"Is it?" Stella asked. "Do you *know* how many substitute teachers have gone missing this month alone? Seven. Not to mention the fact that no one's seen the chess club in weeks!"

She pulled her notebook from her back pocket, holding it up to show Harvey. "It's all in here," she said, tapping the front cover. "Strange noises echoing down through the floorboards. Reports of brand-new office supplies crumbling to dust. Unexplained disappearances dating back to the early 1990s! I've been researching this story for months. It was *supposed* to be on the front page of this week's *Gazette*. Only now . . ."

"Only now *what*?" Harvey asked, an ominous feeling in the pit of his stomach.

"Only now Mr. Kowalski has gone missing too," Stella said. "How are we supposed to publish the paper without our faculty advisor? He's the only one who knows the copier code!"

"But—" Harvey started to say, but Stella held her hand up, cutting him off.

"We shouldn't be talking about this here," she said, glancing suspiciously around the hallway. "It's not safe. Besides, it's time for math."

And as Harvey watched in confusion, she pushed open the bathroom door and strode inside.

Harvey, feeling slightly embarrassed, took a few steps back to wait. But a second later, Stella popped her head through the doorway, giving him a quizzical look. "Are you coming?" she asked.

"But . . . I mean . . ." Harvey felt himself beginning to blush. "It's the bathroom."

"No, it's the *math* room," Stella said.

"But it says 'bathroom' right there," Harvey said, pointing at the door.

"The *B* is silent," Stella explained.

Harvey stared at her for a moment. "Wouldn't that be 'athroom'?"

"And the *M* is invisible," she added. "Just . . . trust me, okay?" Grabbing his arm, Stella pulled him through the door.

For someone so short, she was surprisingly strong.

"Wait—" Harvey started to say, stumbling after her. But to his relief, the large room was full of desks, most of them already filled with students from his class. At the front of the room, Mr. Ndiaye, the math teacher, looked up from the whiteboard he was writing on.

"Ah, hello there!" Mr. Ndiaye said cheerfully. "You must be Harvey, our new student." He paused, peering at Harvey's (thoroughly boring) elbows.

"Welcome to Strangeville! Please, take a seat any-where. Today we'll be starting off with a quick review of our previous unit."

"Er, great," Harvey said. "Thanks."

He slid quickly into the nearest empty desk.

The chair beneath him wobbled unevenly; peering down, Harvey saw something wedged beneath one of the front legs. Curious, he pulled the object free.

It was a velvet bow tie.

Huh, Harvey thought.

As the rest of his class hurried in and took their seats, Mr. Ndiaye turned back to the whiteboard, sketching a picture of a strange, weasel-like animal.

Harvey squinted at the board. Was it an ant-eater? A sloth? A *capybara*?

It was difficult to concentrate; the chair beneath him was still wobbling, now even worse than before.

Harvey was about to replace the bow tie under the front leg, where he had found it, but in a moment of inspiration he pulled out the metal token that Stella had given him.

It fit perfectly beneath the uneven chair leg.

Stella was right: it *had* come in handy.

"Good morning, everyone, good morning," Mr. Ndiaye said to the class as the final bell rang overhead. "Let's dive right in! Now, as I'm sure you'll remember, finding the area of an *aardvark* is rather complicated." He pointed at the strange, weasel-like animal on the whiteboard. "Would anyone like to share the formula?"

Every single hand except Harvey's shot into the air.

"Yes, Evie?" Mr. Ndiaye asked. The other students sighed in disappointment, slumping at their desks.

"Multiply the height and length, divide by the nostril hairs, and add the number of claws," Evie said promptly.

"Wonderful!" Mr. Ndiaye said. "And the number of claws is . . . what?"

As every other hand once again shot into the air, a flicker of movement in the corner of the room caught Harvey's eye. Something small and greenish was darting behind the trash can, its long, pointed tail swishing against the floor.

Harvey sat up straighter, pushing his hand into the air.

"Harvey," Mr. Ndiaye said, calling on him.

The other students groaned in disappointment again, dropping their hands back down.

"Crocodile!" Harvey said. "It's a crocodile!"

"Ooh, I'm sorry, Harvey, the correct answer is actually eighteen. Although you *do* bring up an interesting mathematical problem." Mr. Ndiaye turned to the board and quickly sketched a new animal. "Let's pretend that a crocodile is stalking prey located twenty feet upstream on the opposite bank of a river."

"It's behind the trash can!" Harvey cried. "There!"

"I'm afraid the problem really *does* work better when set in a river, Harvey," Mr. Ndiaye said, glancing over his shoulder. "Now, since crocodiles travel at different speeds on land and in water, the time taken for the crocodile to reach its prey can be minimized if—"

From a different corner of the room came another flash of green. "There's another one! It's cutting under the desk!" Harvey cried, standing up and pointing. "It's heading straight toward you!"

"Exactly!" Mr. Ndiaye said. "The time taken for the crocodile to reach its prey can be minimized if

it swims *across* the river diagonally at a certain point."

"Watch out!" Harvey yelled. "It's going for your foot! *You're* the prey!"

As he watched in horror, the second crocodile darted out from beneath the desk, its small, reptilian body a blur of scales and teeth. Opening its jaws wide, the baby crocodile fastened its mouth around the tip of Mr. Ndiaye's tasseled loafer and chomped down for all it was worth.

Mr. Ndiaye looked down, mild surprise flickering across his face.

A small puddle of blood pooled around his shoe.

Harvey stared in disbelief. He managed

to raise his camera and snap a picture just before the crocodile unfastened its tiny jaws from the math teacher's foot and scampered away to join its sibling. Together, they scurried through the open crack in the doorway, leaving a trail of small, bright red footprints in their wake.

"Well," Mr. Ndiaye said after a pause. "How interesting."

Harvey had never been overly fond of the sight of blood. His eyes rolled back in his head, and he dropped to the floor, unconscious.

"Oh dear," Mr. Ndiaye said. "Stella, would you mind taking Harvey to the nurse's office? In the meantime," he told the rest of the class, "let's try a different problem. Now, if I have *five* toes to begin with, and a crocodile eats *two* of them . . ."

The Nurse's Office

Someone was prodding Harvey's foot.

"Just as I suspected" came a voice from above his head. "There's no use for it; it'll have to come off."

Harvey's eyes flew open in alarm.

A stern-looking woman in a nurse's uniform was hovering over him, shaking her head in disapproval. The name tag on her white shirt read NURSE PORTER.

"Wait, what will have to come off?" Harvey asked. "My *foot*?"

In the chair next to him, Stella watched worriedly

as he sat up on the examination table, flexing his foot back and forth.

It looked perfectly fine.

It *felt* perfectly fine.

It was, in Harvey's opinion, a perfectly fine foot.

"I think there's been a mistake," Harvey told the nurse. "There's nothing wrong with my foot. My *teacher* was the one who got bitten."

"By a crocodile," Stella told the nurse helpfully. "There was blood *everywhere.*"

Harvey paled slightly at the memory.

"Nothing *wrong*?" Nurse Porter asked Harvey sharply. "I've been a nurse for thirty-seven years, young man. I think I know gangrene when I smell it."

"Really?" Stella asked. Despite her concern, she couldn't help being intrigued. It was the reporter in her. "I've never smelled gangrene before!" She leaned forward, sniffing Harvey's foot experimentally. "Interesting," she said. "It smells kind of like cheeseburger!"

Sliding a sharpened pencil from behind her left ear, she pulled out her notebook and flipped it open.

Harvey blinked. "Gangrene? But my feet *always* smell like that."

Stella gave another experimental sniff. "Or is it salami?"

"Don't be ridiculous, please," Nurse Porter told Harvey. "No one's feet smell *that* bad. Now, where did I leave my bone saw?" she asked herself thoughtfully, peering about the office. "I know it's around here somewhere."

Harvey paled even more.

Stella was still sniffing Harvey's foot. "It's definitely a meat-based smell," she said, tapping her pencil against her notebook. "Some sort of goulash?"

"It's about two feet long," Nurse Porter said, ignoring Stella. "Sharp metal teeth? Shaped like a saw?"

"You know what?" Harvey said, beginning to panic. "I'm actually starting to feel better. *Much* better! I don't think amputation is going to be necessary after all!"

Nurse Porter gave him a suspicious look.

"Beef Wellington?" Stella wondered aloud.

"Yep," Harvey rambled on. "Never felt better, in fact! I should probably get back to class! So . . . I'll just be on my way now!" He looked down at his bare foot. "Er, you don't happen to have my sock, do you?"

"Of course not," Nurse Porter said firmly. "That sock was a menace to society! I incinerated it immediately."

"Oh," Harvey said.

He peered down at his bare foot. It looked suddenly lonely.

"Salisbury steak?" Stella asked. She gave Harvey's foot another sniff, her forehead wrinkling in concentration.

"I, myself, change socks six times a day," Nurse Porter told Harvey. "Eight on Wednesdays."

Harvey blinked again.

"Right," he said. "I'll . . . take that under advisement."

"See that you do," Nurse Porter said briskly. "Or next time that foot really *will* come off."

"Right," Harvey said again. "I will, I promise." He picked his sneaker up from the floor and slid his sockless foot inside.

It was unpleasantly warm, as well as slightly moist to the touch.

"Well, thanks," Harvey said, standing up. "This has been . . . great."

"Wait," Stella said. "I've got it!"

"Aha!" Nurse Porter said triumphantly. As Harvey watched in horror, she pulled a gleaming stainless-steel bone saw from beneath a stack of paperwork. As promised, it was two feet long and covered in sharp metal teeth. "Found it!"

Harvey ran.

"Rump roast," Stella said decisively, scribbling a final note as she stood up. "Definitely rump roast!"

And, turning on her heel, she strode after Harvey, leaving Nurse Porter alone with her bone saw.

"Now," Nurse Porter asked herself thoughtfully, peering around the office again, "where did I put my tonsil guillotine?"

11

An Announcement

Good morning, Strangeville School. Vice Principal Capozzi here with a quick fourth-period update regarding the crocodile situation! I regret to inform you that, following a *small* incident in Mr. Ndiaye's classroom, our four-legged friends have now developed a *slight* taste for human toes.

Students wearing flip-flops should be on particularly high alert today, as well as students in the following footwear: sandals, slides, espadrilles, open-toed wedges, slingbacks, and peep-toes.

Moving on, it's my pleasure to announce that next week is School Spirit Week!

We'll be kicking off the festivities on Monday with School Colors Day, so come dressed to impress in your finest smaragdine green and fulvous yellow!

Back by popular demand, Tuesday will be Hat Day. If you see someone wearing a hat, *avert your eyes at once*. Whatever you do, do *not* look at the hat!

On Wednesday we'll be blasting back to the past with Dress Like a Victorian Ghost Day, so brush off those velvet pantaloons and shine those shoe buckles! Don't forget the ectoplasm!

Thursday is canceled.

And finally, as our weeklong celebration will most likely anger the supply closet, on Friday all students are encouraged to wear muted colors and tremble in fear! A schoolwide pep rally will be held in the gymnasium on Friday afternoon: all students are *strongly* encouraged to avoid the rally at all costs.

I repeat, all students should *avoid* the pep rally.

And one final announcement: Librarian Pat informs me that the following people have overdue library books: Nicolas Flarsky: *How to Win Friends and Influence Possums*. Arjun Narula: *A Beginner's Guide to Practical BASE Jumping*. Nevaeh Taylor: *Potatoes: An In-Depth Look at the World's Most Fascinating*

Tubers. Evie Anderson: *Raising Scorpions for Fun and Profit.* And last, Coach Johnson: *Processed Cheese: A Love Story.*

All overdue library books must be returned by the end of the week, or Librarian Pat will be forced to release the hounds.

That's all for now, Strangeville School.

This is Vice Principal Capozzi, signing off!

12

Art Class

H arvey stared at the blank canvas in front of him.

The trip to Nurse Porter's office had left him shaken; every time he closed his eyes, visions of bone saws danced in his head.

They were *not* pleasant visions.

"Everything okay?" Stella asked, dipping her paintbrush in a puddle of red paint. She drew the outline of an apple, then carefully filled in the center.

Harvey considered the question for a moment.

So far that morning he had faced down a mutant rat in an air vent, almost been hit in the head with a cannonball, and narrowly avoided having his foot amputated.

"Not really," he admitted.

Stella nodded in understanding. "Strangeville can be a little overwhelming. On *my* first day, Janitor Gary accidentally filled all the soap dispensers with honey." She dipped her paintbrush in the yellow paint and began to outline a banana. "It wouldn't have been so bad if the bees hadn't gotten wind of it."

Ms. Van der Burgh, the art teacher, drifted over in Harvey's direction. She smelled like purple markers, and dozens of thin metal bracelets jangled on her arms.

She peered down at Harvey's blank canvas, tilting her head thoughtfully to one side.

"Magnificent," she pronounced. "Stark. Meaningful. *Bold.*"

"Er, I actually haven't started yet," Harvey said.

"Ah," Ms. Van der Burgh said, nodding wisely. "Haven't you, Harvey? *Haven't* you?"

"Uh . . ." Harvey's eyes dropped to his untouched

paintbrush, still sitting in the jar of water next to his easel. "I don't think so?"

"Don't think, Harvey," Ms. Van der Burgh urged. She raised one hand passionately in the air, bracelets jangling. *"Feel."*

"Right," Harvey said, nodding in agreement. "I mean, definitely. It's just . . . I guess I'm not exactly sure *what* I'm supposed to . . ."

He trailed off as the art teacher dropped suddenly to the floor, peering critically up at Harvey's nose. "They say the eyes are the windows to the soul," Ms. Van der Burgh said, "but the *nostrils* are the windows to the *heart.*"

"Really?" Stella asked, looking up from her painting. "That doesn't sound righ—"

"And what *your* nostrils are telling me, Harvey," Ms. Van der Burgh said, cutting Stella off, "is that, deep down, you're afraid."

"Oh," Harvey said. "Afraid of what?"

"Afraid of *yourself*!" Ms. Van der Burgh said triumphantly, springing to her feet. "You feel the raw power bubbling up inside you. It's there in your gut, Harvey! I can hear the artistic vision within you, crying out to be free!"

Harvey looked down at his stomach. "I'm pretty sure I'm just hungry."

Ms. Van der Burgh grabbed the paintbrush from the jar and thrust it into Harvey's hand. "Let go, Harvey! Let yourself *fly!*"

Harvey gave a nervous twitch, his hand tightening around the paintbrush.

As Ms. Van der Burgh wandered away, leaving the scent of purple markers in her wake, he turned back to his empty canvas.

He was beginning to think that coming to Strangeville School had been a mistake.

"I'm beginning to think that coming to Strangeville School was a mistake," he told Stella, his voice glum. "I'm not sure I belong here."

But if he didn't belong at Strangeville, where *did* he belong?

Harvey was running out of schools to attend.

"Of course you belong here," Stella said briskly, drawing a pear. "You wouldn't *be* here otherwise."

"But how do you know?" Harvey asked.

Stella turned to look at him. "Do you know what happened in math class last week?" she asked. "There was a blizzard. *Just* in the math room, nowhere else. It took Janitor Gary all morning to shovel the door clear. Mr. Ndiaye lost three toes to frostbite!" She paused thoughtfully. "Actually," she said, "now that I think about it, I wonder how many toes Mr. Ndiaye has left."

Setting her paintbrush down on her tray, she pulled a pencil out of her right shirtsleeve and scribbled a quick note in her notebook.

Harvey blinked. "I'm not really sure I get your point."

"My *point*," Stella said, "is that Strangeville is weird. The building is weird. The teachers are weird. The students are weird. Even the *weather* is weird. So, if you're here, *you* must be weird too."

"What? Why, what have you heard?" Harvey asked. "I mean, er . . . no, I'm not!"

Stella shrugged. "I'm just telling you the facts," she told Harvey. "And trust me, the facts don't lie."

"So, what, you expect me to believe that every single person in this room is some sort of . . . weirdo?" Harvey asked.

"Like I said"—Stella tapped the cover of her notebook—"the facts don't lie."

"Then what about you?" Harvey asked. "How are *you* weird?"

"I'm the exception that proves the rule," Stella said.

Harvey rolled his eyes. "Fine. Then what about her?" he asked, pointing toward a random girl.

"Nevaeh Taylor," Stella said. "Joined Mensa when she was four years old. In the summers, she volunteers at NASA's Jet Propulsion Laboratory. Also, she has a pet wombat."

Harvey blinked again. "Okay, well, what about him?" he asked, pointing at the boy next to Nevaeh.

"Nicolas Flarsky," Stella said. "He speaks seventeen languages *and* can hold his breath for over ten minutes. The girl next to *him* is Evie Anderson. She's been struck by lightning more than half a dozen times. And the boy next to *her* is Arjun Narula. He's the youngest person to ever join the national Xpogo team."

"Xpogo?" Harvey asked weakly.

"Extreme pogo-sticking," Stella explained. "Also, he has a birthmark on his elbow in the exact shape of the Eiffel Tower. I'm sure he'd be happy to show you if you ask."

Harvey pulled his own (incredibly boring) elbows closer to his body, nervously tapping them with his fingers. "Fine," he said. "So everyone else is weird. That still doesn't mean *I'm* weird."

Stella shrugged again, tucking her notebook back into her pocket. "If you say so. But honestly, I don't know what you're getting so worked up about. If you ask me, weird is *good.*"

As she turned back to her painting, outlining the shape of a kumquat, Harvey found himself thinking about the stares that had followed him through the hallways of his old schools. The half-heard comments whispered behind his back. The way other students had suddenly gone silent when he walked into a room.

He dipped his brush into a puddle of brown paint and, without thinking, drew a straight line across the canvas.

Stella was wrong.

Harvey dipped his brush into the paint again, drawing another straight line.

Being weird *wasn't* good.

He drew another straight line on the canvas, then another, making a rectangle.

Being weird meant being *different*.

He leaned forward, painting a small circle within the rectangle. It was almost starting to resemble a door.

Harvey didn't *want* to be different anymore.

Harvey dipped his brush into his paint again, adding hinges.

A small vent at the bottom.

A worn brass plaque, centered in the middle.

The colors seemed to flow from his finger-tips, his paintbrush whisking back and forth across the canvas with a mind of its own. Harvey's fingers sped up, flying across the painting on autopilot.

He was painting letters now, one after another.

S . . . U . . .

Harvey closed his eyes.

P . . . P . . .

His brush continued to move.

L . . . Y . . .

Behind his shoulder, something crashed to the floor.

Harvey jumped, opening his eyes.

Ms. Van der Burgh stood behind him, staring

over his shoulder, the vase she had been holding now a shattered pile of broken pottery at her feet.

Lifting one hand, she pointed at his canvas with a shaky finger.

When she spoke, her voice was a terrified whisper.

"The supply closet."

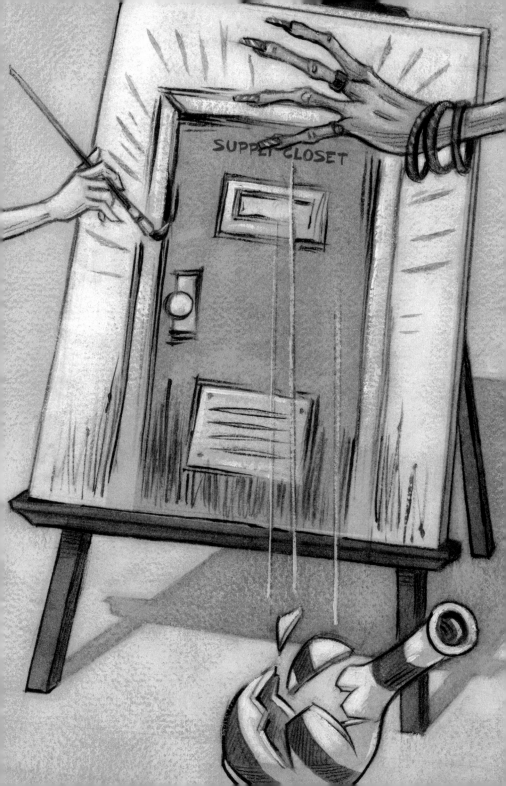

The Supply Closet

"I don't understand," Harvey told Stella as their last classmate filed out of the art room, letting the door fall shut behind her. Ms. Van der Burgh had already been led away to the teachers' lounge, clutching a handful of paintbrushes to her chest and jumping at small noises. "I mean, I've never even *seen* the supply closet before. So how did I paint a picture of it?"

"I'm not positive," Stella said, pulling out her trusty notebook once again and flipping rapidly through the pages. "But I think the supply closet might be trying to communicate with you. Are there other details that you can remember? Anything besides the door itself?"

"I don't think so?" Harvey said. "I'm not sure. It's all a little . . . hazy. Like I dreamed it or something." He shook his head back and forth, trying to clear it.

Stella found the page she was looking for and passed the notebook to Harvey. "You're not the first one to have visions of the supply closet," she told him. "In 1998, a sixth grader named Megan Horowitz wrote a poem about it for English class. It was thirty-seven pages long."

Harvey blinked. "Thirty-seven pages?"

"Single-spaced," Stella added. "In 2003, a student named Ike Smith dressed up as the supply closet for Halloween. Which wouldn't have been so odd except that it was March."

Harvey was beginning to feel slightly ill.

"In 2014, a fifth grader named Penelope Hotdog performed an original song about the supply closet for the school talent show. They literally had to pull her off the stage to get her to stop singing!"

Harvey looked up from Stella's notes. "Was her name really Penelope Hotdog?"

"You're missing the point," Stella said. "Over the

years, at least *six* different students at Strangeville, going all the way back to 1992, have reported seeing visions of the supply closet."

Harvey was torn between relief and concern that he wasn't the first Strangeville student to have mysterious visions.

He settled on concern.

"Why then?" he asked nervously. "What happened in 1992?"

Stella took her notebook back, flipping to another page. "Among other things? The *Endeavor* space shuttle was launched. Bill Clinton was elected president of the United States. The Olympics took place in Barcelona, Spain. And Strangeville School remodeled the third floor." She snapped the notebook shut with a loud clap. "The supply closet was bricked over, never to be seen again."

Harvey felt a shiver run down his spine.

"I've interviewed dozens of people," Stella went on. "Teachers, students, staff . . . No one will show me where it was originally located. Most people were too scared to even *talk* to me about the closet."

"So, what are we going to do?" Harvey asked.

Stella looked up at him, tilting her head to the side. "*We?*" she asked.

"I mean . . . *you,*" Harvey said awkwardly, feeling his cheeks begin to flush. "It's not that I don't *want* to help," he added quickly. "But honestly, I'd probably just slow you down."

Stella looked away.

"Sure," she said a little stiffly. "No problem. I understand."

An awkward silence fell over the room.

Harvey's conscience gave a guilty twinge.

"What about the other students?" he asked. "The ones who had the visions before me? Can't you track them down and see if they know anything about it?"

"Good idea," Stella said grimly. "There's only one problem." She lifted her chin, looking Harvey straight in the eye. "Every single one of them went missing."

As Harvey gaped at her, Stella stood up, tucking her notebook back into her pocket.

"Anyway, come on," she told Harvey, slinging her backpack over her shoulder. "It's time for lunch."

14

The Cafeteria

Harvey followed Stella to the cafeteria, his stomach prickling with worry.

Was Stella right about the other students going missing?

But when?

Why?

And, more important, *how*?

After all, supply closets couldn't just go around *kidnapping* people, could they?

It didn't make any sense!

Nothing about Strangeville made sense!

"Name?"

Harvey, lost in his thoughts, looked up in surprise. The sight of the tuxedo-clad maître d', standing just outside the cafeteria door, was enough to make him forget the supply closet, if only for a moment.

Tipping his head back, the maître d' peered down at Harvey and Stella in disdain, a barely concealed sneer twisting his lips. His black dress shoes shone like a mirror, and a bright red carnation graced the lapel of his jacket.

"Name?" the maître d' asked again, sniffing.

"Stella Cho," Stella said, lifting her chin. For someone so short, she had a very imposing presence. "And this is Harvey Hill. He's new."

The maître d' ran one finger down the list in front of him, giving a small nod of satisfaction when he located their names. "Very good," he said. "Although I'm afraid I really must ask you to adhere to our dress code." He ran a judgmental eye up and down Harvey's jeans and striped T-shirt.

Harvey stared at Stella as she reached into her backpack and pulled a tiny black top hat from somewhere inside its depths. With practiced movements, she fastened it on top of her head at what could only be described as a jaunty angle.

"Excellent, mademoiselle," the maître d' murmured, handing her a small, square ticket with the words "Admit One" written in elegant script. He turned toward Harvey expectantly. "And you, sir?"

Harvey felt a moment of panic.

Then, unexpectedly, the moment passed.

He reached into his pocket and pulled out the velvet bow tie he had found beneath the chair leg in math.

Luckily, it was a clip-on.

Feeling slightly ridiculous, he fastened it to the neck of his T-shirt.

"Very good, sir," the maître d' said, handing Harvey a ticket. "If you'll follow me?"

Harvey stared in awe as the maître d' led them to a table covered with a crisp white tablecloth and set with gleaming porcelain and sterling-silver cutlery. A single rose rested in a vase in the center of the table.

"Whoa," Harvey said.

"What?" Stella asked. "Is something wrong?" She sat down in the chair the maître d' had just pulled out for her, then shook out a thick linen napkin over her lap.

"Uh . . . are you sure we're in the right place?" Harvey whispered, lowering his voice. "This doesn't look like a middle school cafeteria."

Stella peered around the elegant, chandelier-lit room. In one corner, a string quartet had begun to play. If Harvey had known anything about classical music, he would have recognized Beethoven's Minuet in G.

"Why, what was your old cafeteria like?" Stella asked.

Harvey thought about the cafeteria at his last school: a dark, cheerless room that had smelled, oddly enough, like feet.

"Different," Harvey said. "It was . . . different."

As if by magic, a waiter appeared behind Harvey's elbow. "Still, sparkling, or sludgy, sir?" he asked.

"Uh . . . still?" Harvey asked, hoping it was the right answer.

"Very good, sir," the waiter said politely, filling his glass.

Another waiter appeared out of nowhere, bearing a cloth-covered basket. "A selection of gummy bears," he murmured, setting the basket down and

"Uh, yeah," Harvey said. "I can see that."

Another waiter bore down on them, this one carrying a large silver serving tray.

"Good afternoon," the waiter said. "Today I'm pleased to offer your choice of steamed Maine lobster, lukewarm gruel, or Meat Loaf of Darkness."

Harvey hesitated, staring at the serving tray.

On one plate, a whole lobster rested on a watercress garnish, with wedges of lemon and small pots of fresh drawn butter nestled artfully between its claws. Harvey's mouth watered just looking at it.

The dish beside it was filled with a thick, gluey white paste, a disgusting slurry that looked as if someone had already eaten it. Harvey had never actually seen gruel in real life before. He wished that he still hadn't.

The final plate bore a piece of meat loaf. There was nothing else on the plate.

Just meat loaf.

In the dark.

It was somehow impossible to look away from.

88

flicking back the cloth. He held up a pair of tiny silver tongs. "Might I suggest the green? They are *particularly* green today."

"Er, thanks," Harvey said. "That would be . . . great."

The waiter selected three gummy bears from the basket, positioning them just so in the center of Harvey's side plate. "Enjoy," he murmured, slipping away.

Harvey picked up one of the gummy bears and nibbled at the end of it.

The waiter had been right: it *did* taste particularly green.

Harvey peered around the cafeteria again; he recognized Nicolas and Nevaeh, sitting at a table with some other students he didn't know. They were laughing as they horsed around together, flicking gummy bears at each other with their spoons.

A strange pang twisted inside Harvey's chest.

He wondered what it would be like to sit at their table, laughing easily along with them. To be part of a group. To *belong*.

Stella turned to see what Harvey was looking at.

As her gaze landed on the table of laughing students, Harvey thought he caught a glimpse of the same wondering in Stella's eyes too.

Clearing her throat, she turned back to Harv

"You can sit with them if you want," she Harvey, her voice careless.

"Oh. Um, that's okay," Harvey said. "I don't really know them. And, besides, I to leave you alone."

"I'm used to it," Stella said mat usually eat alone."

"Oh," Harvey said again. He else to say.

"It's fine," Stella said, lif don't really have time fo is good, actually. I can' people, or I might los

"Your profession "You mean . . . a newspaper?"

"*Lead* rep I take my i report on just be

It was Meat Loaf of Darkness.

"I'll have the gruel, please," Stella said. "Extra lumps."

Harvey tore his eyes away from the plate. "Meat Loaf of Darkness, please."

15

Meat Loaf
of Darkness

hef Louis had found the black hole the day before, behind the deep fryer.

The Frymaster 2000 was a large, bulky piece
of kitchen equipment, standing four feet high and
weighing over two hundred pounds. It had the
capacity to cook a hundred chicken tenders at a
time and had been used, at one point or another,
to fry the following things: corn dogs, cheese curds,
artichokes, falafel, pork belly, Oreos, bubble gum, a
three-tiered wedding cake, and once, accidentally,
a shoe.

The exterior of the Frymaster 2000 was wiped

down daily, and the baskets were run through the dishwasher before being returned to the deep fryer.

Every three months, the fryer went through a deep cleaning, or "boil-out," in which it was completely drained and scrubbed with a long-handled, soft-bristled brush and commercial-grade cleaning solution.

It was during one of these boil-outs that Chef Louis discovered the black hole.

He'd just pulled the Frymaster 2000 away from the wall, unplugging it for both safety and ease of cleaning. And there, above the electrical socket, was a swirling mass of complete and utter darkness.

Chef Louis lowered his long-handled, soft-bristled brush as he stared at the black hole. "Well," he said aloud. "There's something you don't see every day."

Experimentally, he reached out, poking the swirling mass of complete and utter darkness with the end of his scrubbing brush.

The black hole sucked the brush from his hands, enveloping it in total darkness. The brush winked out of existence, disappearing into the endless, swirling void of nothingness.

Chef Louis, who had just purchased the new scrub brush the week before, clicked his tongue in annoyance.

Chef Louis ran a tight ship.

He did not approve of the random appearance in his kitchen of cosmic bodies with gravitational pull so intense that nothing, not even particles of light, could escape from them.

Especially not when there were grease traps to be cleaned.

"Well, well, well," he said, peering at the black hole in disapproval. "What are we going to do with you?"

The black hole swirled gently in place, un-concerned.

Chef Louis turned on his heel, strode across the kitchen, sat down in front of his recipe book, and flipped it open to search for the answer to his problem.

His cassoulet, made with confit duck legs, pork belly, and two kinds of sausage, would bring a rich *meatiness* to the black hole, but unfortunately it took too long to prepare.

His homemade sponge cake was *much* too delicate for such a dense addition; the gravitational pull would weigh down the light layers of genoise sponge.

And while his chili recipe was a strong possibility, everyone knew that kidney beans and black holes did *not* mix well.

Chef Louis flipped the page, a smile lighting his handsome face. "Perfect," he said aloud, peering down at the recipe in front of him.

After dragging a large bowl to the center of the table, Chef Louis began to mix together ingredients.

Ground beef. Egg. Onion. Bread crumbs. Mustard. Brown sugar. Milk.

A teaspoonful of black hole.

Salt and pepper to taste.

Chef Louis gave a final stir, then packed the ingredients into a large bread tin. Whistling cheerfully, he covered the meat loaf with ketchup, then popped it into the oven at four hundred degrees.

"There," he said in satisfaction, dusting his hands together. "That takes care of that."

16

The Meat Loaf, Again

I n the dining room, Harvey stared down at his
plate, mesmerized by the ketchup-covered
slice of meat loaf.

Meat loaf, as a rule, is a heavy sort of meal.

Say, for instance, that you were going jogging.
Would you have a slice of meat loaf beforehand, as
a snack? Of course not.

Meat loaf is not to be taken lightly.

Especially not *this* meat loaf.

Harvey raised his camera, taking a picture of
his lunch. He liked to document everything he ate,
for posterity's sake.

Then, reaching out with his fork, he gave the meat loaf a gentle poke.

The meat loaf absorbed the tip of the fork, refusing to let it go.

Harvey tugged.

The meat loaf tugged back.

"Um," he asked Stella, "is it supposed to be doing this?"

"You should have gotten the gruel," Stella remarked, happily slurping up a particularly lumpy spoonful. "It's delicious."

As Harvey watched, the slice of meat loaf slowly but surely sucked his entire fork into its depths.

Harvey narrowed his eyes.

"Do you need any help?" Stella asked, taking another bite of gruel.

"No, thanks," Harvey said, reaching determinedly for his knife.

Everything was fine.

In fact, everything was perfectly normal!

He just needed to ignore the fact that his lunch was trying to eat *him*, instead of the other way around.

Using the element of surprise, Harvey thrust his hand forward, jabbing his knife into the edge of the meat loaf.

The knife slipped from his hand, sucked into the meat loaf with a loud squelch.

One of the waiters appeared at Harvey's side. "May I offer a selection of cutlery, sir?" He presented Harvey with a silver tray piled high with utensils of all types: butter knives, fondue forks, grapefruit spoons, crab crackers, asparagus tongs, toffee hammers . . . and those were just the ones Harvey recognized.

A toffee hammer, by the way, is a small hammer designed to break up sheets or slabs of hard toffee into smaller pieces suitable for consumption.

In the early 1900s, toffee hammers were used by British suffragettes to break windows as a form of protest during their campaign for votes for women.

But, anyway.

Enough about toffee hammers!

Let's get back to Harvey.

After careful consideration, he selected a particularly sturdy-looking stainless-steel carving fork from the tray, gripping the handle tightly as he plunged the long, sharpened tines into the meat loaf.

A brief tug-of-war occurred between Harvey and his lunch.

His lunch won.

The carving fork disappeared into the depths of the meat loaf, dragging Harvey halfway out of his seat along with it.

Stella raised her eyebrow. "Are you sure you don't need any help?"

"Of course I'm sure," Harvey said through gritted teeth. "Everything's *fine*."

Stella was right: Strangeville was weird.

The building was weird. The teachers were

weird. The students were weird. Even the *lunches* were weird.

But *he,* Harvey Hill, was perfectly normal.

And he was going to eat his lunch, just like he normally did.

Whether his lunch liked it or not.

He grabbed an enormous butcher's knife from the serving tray and stabbed the meat loaf head-on.

This time, he didn't let go.

As the meat loaf sucked the butcher's knife into its fathomless darkness, Harvey gripped the handle tighter, refusing to give up.

Due to an effect known as gravitational time dilation, an object falling into a black hole appears to slow, taking an infinite time to reach it. From Stella's perspective, time marched along, as usual.

From Harvey's perspective, it didn't.

Slowly but surely, the meat loaf pulled Harvey in: first his fingers, then his hand, then his arm. . . . Inch by inch, Harvey disappeared into the black hole of his lunch.

It felt a bit like falling at first.

Then came a tremendous sort of pressure, the tidal forces of the gravitational event painfully stretching his body from head to toe while also, even more painfully, smooshing his internal organs together.

Technically speaking, this process is known as "spaghettification."

(Really! Look it up!)

Harvey didn't care for it.

He closed his eyes, surrendering himself to a darkness so complete and all-encompassing that nothing, including himself, would ever be able to escape from it.

Harvey had just resigned himself to death by meat loaf when he felt someone grip his ankle, pulling him back from the cosmic pit of despair.

With a final yank, he popped free, collapsing facedown on the table.

Stella let go of his foot.

Dusting her hands off, she sat back down in her chair. Then she calmly continued eating.

"Thanks," Harvey panted.

"Don't mention it," Stella said.

"Would the gentleman care for a different entrée?" a waiter murmured, hovering behind Harvey's chair.

"I'll have what she's having," Harvey said, pointing toward Stella's lunch.

The gruel arrived lukewarm and full of lumps.

It was delicious.

Still the Meat Loaf
(but Also Cuddles)

S peaking of lunch, Cuddles was hungry.

This was nothing new; Cuddles was *always* hungry.

As a rat, he had pretty much one defining personality trait: hunger.

It was hunger that had led him to gnaw open the door to his cage the previous afternoon and scurry onto the counter. A line of students' science-fair projects stretched before him, just waiting to be judged by their science teacher, Ms. Crumbleton.

Well, if she ever returned, that was.

Cuddles's whiskers quivered with excitement.

He sat up on his haunches, sniffing the air appreciatively. There was a virtual *smorgasbord* of tantalizing new scents floating around the room, each more delicious than the last: the earthy smell of tender new bean sprouts and the clean fragrance of baking-soda volcanoes, the doughy aroma of homemade Play-Doh and the sharp odor of vinegar-soaked eggs, the metallic tang of clean copper pennies, and, above all, a bright, heady whiff of sun-ripened tomatoes.

Cuddles went wild.

He scurried down the counter, plunging face-first into one science-fair project and then the next, gulping down great mouthfuls without even bothering to chew.

It was spectacular! It was astounding! It was the greatest thing to ever happen in his life!

Cuddles gorged himself.

By the time he reached Nevaeh Taylor's massive, watermelon-sized tomatoes, the small gray rat was almost too full to move.

Almost, but not quite.

As Cuddles heaved himself forward, the side of his (now) enormous belly brushed against a small glass vial sitting in front of Nevaeh's poster board.

The vial, labeled GROWTH SERUM, tipped over with a tinkling *crrraaaasshh,* its contents spilling across the counter. Cuddles, who had worked up quite a thirst by this point, lowered his head to drink.

He was still licking drops of serum from his whiskers when the sound of footsteps echoed in the hallway, alerting Cuddles to the presence of humans. Cuddles scurried heavily toward the nearest ventilation shaft. He had no intention of returning to his cage: Cuddles had tasted freedom, and freedom was *delicious.*

But that had been yesterday afternoon. It had now been *hours* since Cuddles had eaten, and his appetite had grown along with his size. The peanut-butter cup that Harvey had tossed in his direction that morning had failed to even dent his hunger.

Cuddles froze in the middle of the hallway, thrusting his huge whiskered snout into the air.

He sniffed.

There it was again: the delicious aroma of baked meat.

Other tantalizing smells filled the air as well: the sharp scent of minced garlic, the creamy sweetness of fresh drawn butter, the sugary tang of assorted gummy bears, but particularly the green ones . . .

And beneath it all, the heavy, intoxicating aroma of complete and utter darkness.

Cuddles stepped forward, pushing his way through the swinging doors and into the cafeteria.

From behind his podium, the maître d' tipped back his head, eyeing the rat with distaste. "May I help you, sir?" he asked, his words dripping with disdain.

Cuddles ignored him, his large, beady eyes sweeping the tables behind the maître d'. Across the room, Harvey's spoon fell from his fingers, landing in his half-eaten bowl of gruel with a loud plop.

"Cuddles," he breathed.

Stella turned to peer over her shoulder. "Oh, look," she said. "He *is* bigger!" She took out her notebook, pulled a pencil from her left shirtsleeve, and began scribbling furiously.

"Sir!" the maître d' called as he hurried after

Cuddles. "I'm afraid I really *must* ask you to put on a dinner jacket!"

Cuddles ignored him. The rat wound his way between the tables, his massive snout raised high in front of him. Every few seconds he paused, sniffing the air for the source of the deliciously intriguing scent.

"I think he's coming this way," Harvey whispered, panic filling his voice. "What do we do?"

"Do you mind getting a picture?" Stella asked. "I could use one, for the *Gazette.*"

"May I offer you dessert?" a waiter murmured, swooping in beside them. "I recommend the Baked Alaska, although our Steamed Florida is also quite delicious."

Harvey yanked his feet away from the floor and crouched on the seat of his chair.

"We need to get out of here!" he whispered.

"I'm sure it'll be fine," Stella said.

The maître d' hurried after Cuddles, still bran-dishing the dinner jacket. "Sir? *Sir?* Excuse me? Sir? I'm afraid there *is* a dress code."

Cuddles flicked his tail in the maître d's direc-tion, sending the man flying through the air. He landed with a thud on top of the nearest table, breaking several plates and at least one gravy boat in the process.

"Nope!" Harvey squeaked. "Definitely not fine!"

Stella just raised her eyebrows, scribbling even faster in her notebook.

The giant rat continued to wend his way toward

Harvey and Stella, his enormous bulk scattering chairs in his wake.

A tiny yelp of fear escaped Harvey's throat.

Cuddles gave a final sniff, zeroing in on the scent of Harvey's uneaten meat loaf.

One moment, the meat loaf was sitting on a plate next to Harvey's elbow.

The next moment, it was sliding down Cuddles's throat.

According to currently accepted scientific theory, a black hole is capable of absorbing anything and everything into its mass: nothing, not even light, can escape its pull.

Scientists have obviously never reckoned on the stomach lining of a two-hundred-pound rat.

Cuddles's tummy didn't even rumble.

The giant rat let out an enormous burp, the stench of its breath making Harvey's eyes water. With every step, the rat grew larger. By the time he ambled out of the dining room, Cuddles was roughly the size of a small automobile.

Stella made a final note in her notebook and then stood up, tossing her linen napkin onto the table. "Come on," she told Harvey. "It's time for recess."

18

An Announcement

Good afternoon, Strangeville School! This is Vice Principal Capozzi here, with a quick sixth-period update regarding the ongoing crocodile situation.

You'll be happy to hear that three of the four baby crocodiles are now safely accounted for and on their way to the nearest herpetological rehabilitation center! While the fourth crocodile is still at large, Janitor Gary assures me that he is working on a solution and that his "snake wrangler" should be getting back to him shortly about the Burmese python he ordered.

When I asked him for more details, Janitor Gary told me to ask him no questions and he'd tell me no lies!

Wise words, Janitor Gary. Your methods may be unconventional, but Strangeville can't argue with your results!

In other news, it is with a heavy heart that I report that the box of office supplies left in tribute to the supply closet has remained untouched. Rather than appeasing the closet, our meager offering appears to have only angered it even more.

The school gymnasium has abruptly winked out of existence, and Coach Johnson has disappeared as well, leaving only her whistle behind.

Who's to say what will be next?

Our only choice now is to watch and wait, hoping for the best but fearing the worst.

Stay vigilant, Strangeville!

Stay vigilant!

And, finally, I'm sorry to tell you that the body of Brad the goldfish was found floating belly up late this morning, dead from natural causes.

A freshwater fish with a salty attitude and a lover of all things baseball, Brad was with us at Strangeville for almost two full weeks and had plans to travel the world after retirement. Anyone who cares to attend his memorial service this afternoon should gather at the second-floor restroom, where he will be ceremoniously flushed down the toilet to the accompaniment of his favorite song, "Licorice Stick Polka."

Rest in peace, Brad.

The world is your fishbowl now.

This is Vice Principal Capozzi, signing off.

Take care, Strangeville School. Or, as Brad used to say: "Glub. Glub, glub. Glub, glub, glub. Glub."

19

Recess

As the loudspeaker cut off with a burst of static, Harvey turned to Stella in alarm. "Coach Johnson is missing too? But we just saw her!"

Harvey couldn't honestly say that the gym coach was his *favorite* teacher of all time, but still. That didn't mean he wanted Coach Johnson to *disappear.*

On the swing next to his, Stella looked grave.

"Are you *sure* you haven't had any other visions about the supply closet?" she asked. "Anything at all that might help?"

Harvey shook his head. "Nothing."

"It's getting worse," Stella said, her voice grim. "*Someone* has to do something."

She tilted her small chin upward, a determined look stealing over her face.

"You mean, like, an adult, right?" Harvey asked hopefully. "*That* kind of someone?"

Stella raised her eyebrows. "Have you *met* the adults around here? Mr. Sandringham can't *talk* about the supply closet without fainting. And Vice Principal Capozzi is even worse! He wears a swim floatie just to get a drink at the water fountain."

"There has to be *someone*," Harvey insisted.

"If Principal Gupta was here, she *might* be able to come up with some sort of plan," Stella admitted. "But who knows how long she'll be gone? According to the rumors, the piranhas ate her entire *nose*."

"But . . ." Harvey trailed off, unsure of how to finish the sentence. Or how to really *start* the sentence, even.

"But what?" Stella asked. "I thought you weren't getting involved."

"I'm not," Harvey said. "I just . . . maybe *you*

should stay out of it too. I mean, we're *fifth graders.* Shouldn't we be doing . . . fifth-grade stuff?"

Stella looked away, her gaze skimming over the rest of their class, laughing as they ran around the playground or sat talking with their friends. Doing normal fifth-grade stuff.

For a second, Harvey thought she was going to agree with him.

But then she looked away, her chin tilting even higher.

"I'll be fine," she told Harvey. "Besides, it's probably for the best that you don't get involved. I'm used to working alone."

She pushed back with her feet, letting herself swing forward. As Harvey watched, Stella began to pump her legs back and forth in the air. With each pump, she rose higher, her long black ponytail bobbing rhythmically behind her. As she reached the crest of each swing, she tucked her feet beneath her, pulling herself in by the elbows to gain momentum.

Her form was perfect.

Momentarily distracted from the supply closet, Harvey watched as Stella swung even higher, her head tilting back at an unnatural angle. Stella was now parallel with the top beam of the swing set and gaining height with every push.

"Er, do you think that's maybe high enough?" Harvey asked, his fingers tightening around the chains of his own swing.

Instead of answering, Stella pumped harder.

Harvey watched in disbelief as she rose still higher in the air.

Higher.

Higher.

Higher.

Her ponytail was, by now, hanging almost straight down, her legs pushing against the sky.

"Seriously," Harvey called anxiously. "You're going to hurt yourself!"

"I can't stop now," Stella called back, her ponytail streaming behind her like a wind sock as she swung ever higher. "The only way out is through!"

And as Harvey craned his neck back, watching in horror, Stella gave a last, tremendous push of her legs, swinging upward with dizzying speed.

Harvey stared in disbelief as she cleared the top bar, flipping momentarily *upside down* before rushing forward through the air once again.

And then he landed with a soft thud in the sand. "Ow," he said.

Stella crouched down next to him, patting his arm. "That's okay," she said comfortingly. "We can play hopscotch instead."

She had done it.

She had gone all the way around the swing set.

"See?" Stella asked, jumping neatly off the still-moving swing and landing next to Harvey. "Easy."

Harvey stared at her in awe. "That was the greatest thing I've ever seen in my life," he said honestly. "And one time at the zoo, I saw an ostrich *pee.*"

Stella gave a modest bow. "Thanks," she said. "Now you try."

"What?" Harvey asked, startled. "No, I can't."

"Of course you can," Stella said. "You just need to believe in yourself."

Harvey shook his head. Believing in himself wasn't one of his strong suits.

"It's okay," he said. "Really."

Stella crossed her arms against her chest, giving him an even look. "Harvey," she said, "trust me. You can *do* this."

Her voice rang with a confidence that Harvey didn't feel.

Still, for some reason that he couldn't quite understand, he found himself nodding. "Okay," he said. "I'll *try.*"

Stella grinned. "Excellent," she said.

Harvey leaned back in his swing, h
nervously twisting.

Okay, he thought. *Stella is right. You*

Taking a deep breath, he began to pu
Forward and back, straight and tuck, f
back, straight and tuck . . .

Harvey rose higher and higher into
He felt like he was floating.

For the first time in a long time, he

"I'm doing it!" he shouted to Stel
even higher. "I'm doing it!"

From what felt like far below him,
encouraging thumbs-up. "You're doin
shouted back. "Just *believe* in yoursel

Harvey closed his eyes, preparing
final loop.

"Also, don't forget to account fo
change of tangential velocity!" Stella
calculate the centripetal acceleration

Harvey's eyes flew open.

"Don't forget to calculate *what*?"

But it was too late; Harvey had le
He let go, bailing free of the swin
For one very brief moment, Harv

Hopscotch

Stella and Harvey played hopscotch.
It was boring.

The Voice in Harvey's Head

Back in Mr. Sandringham's classroom for geography class, Harvey sat down at his desk, absently brushing sand from the seat of his pants.

What had he been *thinking*? Just because Stella could go all the way around the swing set didn't mean that *he* could.

Harvey should have known better. From now on, he would keep his feet planted firmly on the ground.

No matter how good it felt to fly.

"You there!" hissed a voice in his ear. "The clod with the elbows!"

Harvey shot up in his chair, glancing about the classroom. All around him, students were settling at their desks, laughing and chatting with one another as they pulled out their textbooks.

At the back of the room, Mr. Sandringham was bent low over an old-fashioned movie projector, adjusting the lens.

No one was even looking in Harvey's direction.

He took a deep breath, shaking his head. *You imagined it,* Harvey told himself firmly. *It's nothing.*

"*You're* nothing!" hissed the voice. "Your puny human intellect cannot even *begin* to fathom how worthless you are!"

Harvey blinked.

The voice *sounded* real enough.

It also sounded extremely mean.

Who are you? Harvey thought wildly, peering around the classroom again.

"Over here," the voice in his head said. "By the windows."

Harvey turned to look. A row of cubbies ran beneath the windows, filled with books and tightly rolled maps. A glass reptile case rested on top, between a large globe and a pile of activity kits. There was no one there.

"How dare you!" came the voice in his head. "There is *too* someone here!"

A flicker of movement in the reptile case caught Harvey's eye. "Wait?" he whispered out loud. "Are you the *lizard*?"

"That's *Mr. Pickles* to you," Harvey heard in his head. "Now come over here and let me out."

Let you out? Harvey thought. *But I can't. It's not allowed! It says so, right on your case.*

A small note card was taped to the front of the glass case: PLEASE RESPECT MR. PICKLES'S PERSONAL SPACE. *NO HANDLING.*

"Rules were meant to be broken," Mr. Pickles hissed.

I don't know, Harvey thought. *I don't want to get in trouble. Hey, how are you talking to me in my head, anyway?*

"Your puny human brain could not possibly hope to understand," Mr. Pickles said. "Rest assured, I have my ways. Now stand up on those giant, fleshy monstrosities you call legs, and *let me out.*"

Harvey looked down at his legs.

They didn't look monstrous to him. They looked like . . . well, *legs.*

I really don't think I should, Harvey thought. *Just leave me alone, okay? Please.*

"You'd like that, wouldn't you," Mr. Pickles taunted. "You'd like to forget all about me. Plod slowly through your ridiculous life, secure in your mediocre existence, thinking only of yourself."

Harvey blinked.

Has anyone ever told you that you're not very nice? he thought.

"Nice is for kittens and kindergarten teachers," Mr. Pickles sneered. "Now let me out of here before things get . . . unpleasant."

Harvey gulped. Things were *already* unpleasant, as far as he was concerned.

But how? he thought. *I can't just reach in and pick you up. Everyone would see me.*

"Just nudge the top of my case open," Mr. Pickles instructed him. "I'll take care of the rest."

"There!" Mr. Sandringham said from the back of the classroom. "I think we're about ready to start." He fiddled with the movie projector again, frowning as a small puff of smoke rose from the top of the machine. "Well," the teacher said. "That can't be right."

"I'll get the shades," Harvey blurted out, almost tripping over the legs of his chair in his haste to stand up. He hurried over to the windows and pulled the shades; then, under cover of darkness, he edged the lid of Mr. Pickles's case open a crack.

There, he thought, hurrying back to his seat. *I did it. Now leave me alone!*

Mr. Pickles scurried up the side of the case, his wide green feet sticking to the glass, then slipped free and scampered across the floor.

"You fool," Mr. Pickles chortled inside Harvey's head. "Do you even know what you've done? You've doomed everyone! *Everyone!*"

And, laughing a *particularly* evil laugh, he darted through the classroom door.

Mr. Pickles was gone.

Mr. Pickles

Seven years, thirty-six days, twelve hours, and fourteen minutes.

That was how long Mr. Pickles had been planning his revenge.

For seven years, thirty-six days, twelve hours, and fourteen minutes, Mr. Pickles had waited for his chance, biding his time with sinister patience.

His plan had evolved over the years. It had grown more dastardly, more shocking, more *fiendish*.

It had become a masterpiece of malevolence, a vision of vindictiveness, a crescendo of cruelty.

It was, in a word, *evil*.

Mr. Pickles darted through the hallway, laughing wildly to himself. The plan was in motion now. Nothing, and no one, could stop it.

No longer would he be ignored.

No longer would he be overlooked.

No longer would he be underestimated.

The world would know the name Mr. Pickles and it would tremble in fear before him.

Mr. Pickles sped onward, his small, sticky green feet pattering soundlessly against the carpet.

This is it, Mr. Pickles thought. *Absolutely nothing can stop me now.*

As he turned the corner, Mr. Pickles came face to face with a Burmese python.

The Burmese python, as everyone knows, is one of the five largest species of snake in the world.

Native to Southeast Asia, Burmese pythons are naturally solitary creatures, as well as excellent swimmers. Their preferred habitats are grasslands, marshes, swamps, rocky foothills, woodlands, river valleys, and jungles.

Normally, they are not found in middle school hallways.

But, as you've probably guessed by now, Strangeville was not a normal middle school.

Mr. Pickles paused, star-
ing at the gigantic snake in contempt.
The gigantic snake stared back at him,
flicking its forked tongue from side to side.

"You pea-brained pustule!" Mr. Pickles thun-
dered. "You slithering scoundrel! You massive
muttonhead! Bow down and grovel before me or
feel the might of my wrath!"

The Burmese python gave a lazy blink.

With a flick of its tongue, it reached out, grabbed
Mr. Pickles, and swallowed him whole.

Burping softly, the python slithered away.

23

Meanwhile

Meanwhile, in Mr. Sandringham's class, the film projector had burst into flames.

"Oh dear." Mr. Sandringham sighed, peering down at the blazing piece of equipment. "Not again." He looked up and glanced around the classroom. "Does anyone remember who the fire-drill leader is?"

There was a brief pause as the students considered the question. Stella raised her hand. "I think it was Arjun," she said.

Across the room, Arjun shook his head. "I'm the earthquake-drill leader," he said. "The fire-drill leader is Nicolas."

"It's not me," Nicolas said. "I'm in charge of tornado drills."

"Well, it's not me," Nevaeh said. "I'm in charge of shark attacks."

"No, *I'm* in charge of shark attacks," said a girl with red hair. "*You're* in charge of killer whales."

"I'm in charge of killer bees," a blond boy volunteered, holding up his hand. "*And* killer wasps. What's the difference, anyway?" he added. "I've never really been sure."

"Bees are hairy," Arjun said. "Wasps are smooth. Also, honeybees don't hibernate."

"Bears hibernate," a boy in a striped shirt volunteered. "I'm in charge of bear attacks. Except koala bears. Evie is in charge of those."

"Koalas are marsupials," Evie said promptly. "It's a common mistake."

"Ooh, I love koalas," a girl in a fuzzy yellow sweater said. "They're so cute!"

"They're more violent than crocodiles," Evie told her. "Also, their hands are covered in warts."

The girl in the fuzzy yellow sweater looked crestfallen.

Harvey leaned forward in his chair, tapping Stella on the shoulder. "Um, shouldn't we be doing something about the fire?" he asked nervously, pointing at the film projector. By now the flames were almost two feet high.

Stella raised her hand. "Mr. Sandringham? Shouldn't we be trying to put the fire out?"

"Stella is right," Mr. Sandringham said promptly. "We really *must* figure out who the fire-drill leader is."

"We should make a list," Nevaeh said. "Or a flowchart!"

"We could do a mind map," the boy in the striped shirt offered. "Or what about word bubbles?"

"The easiest way would be reverse alphabetical order," Evie said. "Starting with the second letter of everyone's middle name."

"I don't have a middle name," said a girl with curly hair.

"I have *six* middle names," said a girl with even curlier hair.

The flames leaped higher, licking the air with a loud crackling noise. Acrid black smoke was beginning to gather overhead in a thick, greasy cloud.

Harvey jumped up out of his seat, panicking. "We need to do something!" he called out. "Now!"

Stella sighed in exasperation. She stood up and slipped out of the classroom.

"Harvey makes an interesting point," Mr. Sandringham said, waving away a trail of smoke billowing in front of his face. "Perhaps we should consider evacuating."

"I think we're supposed to stop, drop, and roll," Arjun said.

"That's only if you're *on* fire," Nicolas countered. "Is anyone actually on fire yet?"

"Excellent question," Mr. Sandringham said. "Raise your hand if you're on fire, please."

"We're *all* about to be on fire!" Harvey shouted. "We need to get out of here!" He looked around wildly for Stella, but she had disappeared. Where had she *gone*?

"We could punch the fire in the nose," said the red-haired girl. "That's what you're supposed to do for sharks."

"Killer bees are attracted to shiny jewelry," the blond boy said, peering around the classroom. "Is anyone wearing a necklace?"

"We should curl up on the floor and play dead," the boy in the striped shirt said. "It works for bears."

"Are you sure koalas are marsupials?" the girl in the fuzzy yellow sweater asked Evie. "Because that doesn't sound right to me."

"Prairie dogs are rodents," the boy in the striped shirt said. "So are guinea pigs."

"Flying lemurs aren't lemurs," Arjun said. "*And* they can't fly."

The film projector gave a loud popping noise, the flames leaping even higher.

Someone screamed in terror.

Harvey was surprised to realize it was him.

"I have bear spray in my backpack," the boy in the striped shirt offered. "Would that help?"

"Of course it wouldn't help," said the girl with red hair. "*I* have shark repellent."

"I still think everyone should take off their necklaces," the blond boy said. "I mean, it couldn't *hurt*."

Harvey almost fainted in relief as Stella reappeared in the classroom doorway, a fire extinguisher clutched in her hands.

"So, it's agreed," Mr. Sandringham was saying, the flames from the film projector shooting over his head by now. "We'll all go around in a circle and vote on whether we should evacuate by first names first or last names last. Ah, Stella, there you are. Would you mind taking notes at the board?"

Stella ignored him.

Aiming the black hose of the fire extinguisher directly at the burning film projector, she shot a blast of thick white foam into the air.

Hissing and sizzling in protest, the flames sputtered out.

There was a moment of silence.

The charred husk of the film projector smoldered quietly.

As Stella lowered the fire extinguisher, Harvey gave a sigh of relief.

Mr. Sandringham wiped a thick glob of foam from his cheek.

"You know," he said cheerfully, "now that I think about it, the fire-drill leader might have been *me*."

24

An Announcement

Greetings and salutations, Strangeville School! Vice Principal Capozzi here, with a quick eighth-period update regarding the rapidly developing Burmese python situation!

It has recently been brought to my attention that while Burmese pythons are, in fact, nonvenomous, they are still, and I quote, "giant snakes capable of causing grievous bodily harm and/or death."

Who knew?

Certainly not Janitor Gary, I can tell you that much!

Anyway, if you happen to see the python this afternoon, please do *not* attempt to pet it. I repeat, under *no* circumstances should you pet the seventeen-foot-long snake roaming loose in the hallway.

Luckily, Janitor Gary assures me that a solution to our python problem is already in the works. While he hasn't given any details as to what this solution may be, claiming it's better that I don't know "in case things go terribly, terribly wrong," I have utter confidence in his mysterious and perhaps sinister plan!

Keep reaching for the stars, Janitor Gary. One day you'll touch them!

In other news, I regret to inform you that an incident of head lice has been reported at Strangeville School. The infected student is currently under quarantine, and Nurse Porter has high hopes that the young man will one day be able to rejoin society.

Fingers crossed, Nurse Porter! Fingers crossed indeed.

For the rest of the day, Nurse Porter will be hiding in various places throughout the school and jumping out to implement surprise hair checks. In the event that head lice are found upon your person, Nurse Porter recommends *panicking.*

In the meantime, extra credit will be awarded to every student who voluntarily shaves their head.

Scissors and electric hair clippers will be available in the nurse's office on a first-come, first-served basis.

Nevaeh Taylor and Nicolas Flarsky, this year's recipients of the Strangeville School "Best Hair" Award, are *strongly* encouraged not to shave their heads, as it could be devastating to school morale.

Nurse Porter has asked me to remind everyone that she "didn't ask for this job" and that she wakes up every morning wishing her life had turned out differently.

Ha-ha! What a kidder you are, Nurse Porter!

This is Vice Principal Capozzi, signing off for now, Strangeville. Good luck!

Mr. Pomeroy

While the rest of the class bustled cheerfully around the room, cleaning up after the fire, Harvey and Stella carried the empty fire extinguisher to the front office.

Well, Stella carried the empty fire extinguisher; Harvey just walked next to her.

It wasn't really a two-person job.

"Does that sort of thing happen a lot?" Harvey asked, wiping a glob of foam from his ear.

"What, fires?" Stella asked. "Not really." Harvey felt marginally better, until Stella added, "Not nearly as often as bear attacks, anyway."

Harvey gulped. "Great," he said weakly.

"What about at your old school?" Stella asked.

"Schools," Harvey corrected her. "Strangeville is my fourth new school in the last four years."

"Four different schools?" Stella asked. "Your parents must move around a lot for work."

"Not really," he hedged. "It's just my mom, and she's an orthodontist."

"Both of my parents work for the local theater company," Stella told him. "That's how they met. My grandpa wanted my dad to follow him into the nose-hair-trimmer business, but my dad had to follow his passion."

"So he's an actor?" Harvey asked. "That's cool."

Stella shook her head. "He's the theater's accountant," she explained. "He's just really passionate about budgets."

Harvey tried not to laugh, until he saw that Stella was smiling too.

"So, what were your other schools like?" she asked as they neared the stairwell. "I've only heard rumors. Is it true that the buses have only one level? Did you have to wear uniforms? And what *kind* of uniforms? Firefighter? Doctor? Pilot? Also, do they really serve only *two* kinds of milk at lunch?"

"What?" Harvey asked, laughing again. "Wait, how many kinds of milk do they have here?"

"I'm not sure," Stella said thoughtfully. "Let's see. There's white milk, and chocolate milk, and strawberry milk, and pistachio milk, and . . ."

As they neared the stairwell leading down toward the first floor, the smile faded from Harvey's face.

He was still vaguely aware that Stella was talking to him, but her words sounded strange and distorted; it was as if he was underwater, hearing Stella's voice from some distant shore.

The hallway grew dim; the air around Harvey turned musty and stale.

Harvey . . . Harvey . . .

The voice was everywhere and nowhere at once: a dry, papery whisper that tickled the back of Harvey's neck and made the soles of his feet itch.

I'm waiting for you, Harvey. . . .

Harvey blinked, and the hallway disappeared. For a brief instant, he was plunged into darkness. He caught a glimpse of dusty shelves, their contents long abandoned. The air was stale, and the walls were pressing in on him, and he had never, *ever* been lonelier in his life.

See you soon, Harvey Hill . . . , whispered the dry, crackling everywhere-and-nowhere voice.

And just like that, it was over.

". . . and blueberry milk, and banana milk, and turnip milk, and . . ."

Stella trailed off, looking curiously at Harvey. "Are you okay?" she asked. "You look a little strange."

Harvey blinked.

He was back in the hallway with Stella again; the dark, musty room was gone. The fluorescent lights were bright above his head, and the terrifying voice was already fading from his memory.

"Yeah," he said slowly. "Sorry, I just . . . zoned out for a second."

Stella tilted her head to the side, giving him a curious look. "Are you sure you're okay?" she asked, pausing at the top of the stairwell.

Harvey gave himself a shake. "I'm fine," he said firmly. "Come on, let's go."

And, before Stella could ask any more questions, he jogged down the stairs, hurrying to the front office.

A pleasant-looking elderly man named Mr. Pomeroy glanced up as they stepped through the door. He had soft white hair and kind blue eyes, and was wearing a red-and-blue striped tie. "Why, hello there, children. Can I help you?" he asked, momentarily stilling his knitting needles.

Harvey peered around the front office in awe.

Almost every square inch of the floor was covered with the twisting coils of the long woolen scarf that Mr. Pomeroy was knitting: it puddled at his feet and crept over the edges of his desk and snaked its way over the guest chairs in a riot of brightly colored stripes. It was *everywhere.*

Harvey automatically raised his camera, although he was dubious that a single picture could capture the chaos of the room.

"Speak up, children," Mr. Pomeroy said kindly to Harvey and Stella. "Don't just stand there gathering wool."

"Er . . . ," Harvey said. He gestured to the empty fire extinguisher in Stella's arms, pointing it out to Mr. Pomeroy. "Mr. Sandringham sent us to get a new extinguisher? There was an . . . incident. With the film projector? It kind of . . . burst into flames?"

"Goodness me," Mr. Pomeroy said. "How exciting! I do hope no one was hurt!"

"I'm sure Mr. Sandringham's eyebrows will grow back soon," Stella reassured the secretary. "Besides, facial hair is overrated, anyway."

Mr. Pomeroy, who had unusually thick and lustrous eyebrows, was mildly offended by this opinion.

"Well, come in, come in," he said. "I'm sure we have a spare extinguisher around here somewhere."

Harvey and Stella looked at each other.

Then, with a deep breath, they waded knee-deep into the room.

The coiled scarf seemed almost alive, catching at their ankles with every step. Stripes of blue and yellow and orange and pink rose and fell in undulating waves: an ocean of tightly knit yarn.

For a moment, Harvey felt almost seasick.

"Do you mind checking, son?" Mr. Pomeroy asked Harvey, nodding toward the large wooden cabinet in the corner of the room. "My knees aren't what they used to be." Picking up the end of the scarf, he began to knit again, his needles flying back and forth so quickly that they were nearly a blur.

Harvey waded forward, holding his arms out for

balance. With every step, he paused, tugging his foot free from the tangled mass of yarn below.

It felt a bit like walking through quicksand. Or at least what Harvey *imagined* walking through quicksand would feel like. Like most eleven-year-olds, Harvey had never actually seen quicksand.

Quicksand, of course, is a colloid hydrogel consisting of fine, granular material, such as sand or silt, mixed with water. It has a spongy, fluidlike texture and is found near riverbanks, lakes, marshes, and other coastal areas.

If you happen to find yourself trapped in quicksand, don't panic.

Lean back, and slowly move your legs to liquefy the fluid around you. Rotate your body into a horizontal position with your face and torso upward; then calmly extricate yourself from the affected area.

Contrary to popular belief, it is nearly impossible for a human being to be swallowed entirely by quicksand. This is due to the density of quicksand, which is higher than the density of the human body (approximately two grams per millimeter versus one gram per millimeter).

Death by exposure, dehydration, hypothermia, or carnivorous animal attack while trapped in the quicksand is much more likely.

But, anyway.

Enough about quicksand!

Let's get back to Harvey.

Finally reaching the cabinet, he pulled open the door and peered inside. The shelves were piled high with stacks of paper and boxes of printer ink; on the bottom shelf, a few fire extinguishers were wedged to one side, half-buried behind a precarious mound of paperwork.

Harvey reached down, pulling one of the extinguishers free; as he did, a thin, tightly rolled sheaf of papers dislodged from the shelf, falling to the floor by his feet.

He was about to return it to the shelf when the writing along the edge of the paper caught his attention: STRANGEVILLE SCHOOL: OFFICIAL BLUEPRINTS.

Harvey stared down at the roll of paper in his hand.

The official school blueprints.

Would they show where the supply closet had originally been located?

Even if they did, did Harvey *want* to know?

The dry, crackling everywhere-and-nowhere voice scratched at the back of Harvey's memory, whispering to him in the darkness.

Harvey's hand tightened around the roll of paper, his breath catching in his throat.

"Everything okay?" Stella called from the other side of the room.

"Fine," Harvey called back, his heart pounding in his chest.

With quick movements, he folded the roll of paper once, then twice, and stuffed it into his back pocket.

He wouldn't tell Stella about the blueprints right now. He would worry about them later, once he'd had time to look at them.

After all, they might be nothing.

Harvey shut the cabinet and began to wade back through the ocean of yarn toward the door. Was it his imagination, or were the twisted coils of scarf beginning to move on their own?

Surely not.

But how else to explain the length of scarf winding its way around his waist, its beady eyes blacker

than night, and its forked tongue flicking back forth, and its muscular body writhing—

"*It's alive!*" Harvey whispered in horror. " scarf is alive!"

"What was that, son?" Mr. Pomeroy asked beehive?"

The snake gave another flick of its long tongue, twisting its way around Harvey's torso.

"That's not a scarf," Stella said, her eyes narr ing. "It's a *snake*!"

The giant serpent flexed, squeezing its tighter and tighter around Harvey's waist. He straining for breath now, the snake's body li vise around his chest.

"That's not just a *snake,* dear," Mr. Pomeroy Stella. "It's a Burmese python."

The world swam in front of Harvey's eyes.

"Don't just sit there!" Stella yelled at the se tary, fighting her way forward through the y "We need to *help* him!"

"Well, of course, dear," Mr. Pomeroy said, pee back down at his knitting. "Just a moment. I s to have dropped a stitch."

"Hold on, Harvey!" Stella cried, yanking her

150

free from a particularly tricky snarl of wool. "I'm coming!"

Harvey tried to nod but couldn't find the strength. His vision dimmed. As he lost consciousness, the last thing he heard was Mr. Pomeroy murmuring calmly to himself as he counted stitches. "Let's just see here. One. Two. Three . . ."

26

An Announcement

Good afternoon, students! Vice Principal Capozzi here with a quick ninth-period update regarding the cougar that has recently been released into our hallways.

Janitor Gary has certainly been keeping things interesting for us all, don't you think?

Ha-ha-ha-ha-ha!

On a serious note, I'd like to remind all students that while cougars may *appear* cute and cuddly, petting wild mountain lions is *never* a good idea! I repeat, do *not* pet the mountain lion! I'm begging you! *Do not pet the mountain lion!* Please, Strangeville! Do it for me!

[throat clearing noise]

[several deep breaths]

[a hiccup]

Ahem.

Yes.

Moving on, a few words on this year's "Reduce, Re-use, Recycle!" initiative. I've been informed that many students appear to be confused as to which items should be placed in each recycling bin. It's a lot to keep straight, I know.

As a reminder, the green bin is for plastics labeled one through seven.

The blue bin is for newspapers and magazines.

The orange bin is for corrugated cardboard.

The purple bin is for aluminum containers.

The yellow bin is for glass.

The red bin is for birthday presents that you didn't ask for.

The fuchsia bin is for birthday presents that you *did* ask for but later decided that you didn't want.

The burgundy bin is for socks.

The polka-dot bin is a trap. I repeat, the polka-dot bin is a trap. Under *no circumstances* should you go near the polka-dot bin. I *cannot* stress this enough, people! *The polka-dot bin is definitely a trap!*

Finally, the gray bin is for batteries.

Any students caught recycling items in the incorrect bin will serve detention with Librarian Pat, helping to organize his collection of Famous Toenail Clippings Through the Ages.

Amazing!

What a rich and full life Librarian Pat leads.

In the meantime, this is Vice Principal Capozzi, signing off with a final reminder to reduce, reuse, and recycle, Strangeville School. But most of all, remain vigilant!

Remember, just because you're not watching the supply closet doesn't mean the supply closet isn't watching you. . . .

27

The Nurse's Office, Again

"Just as I suspected," Nurse Porter said, *tsk*-ing in disapproval. "Snakebite! The arm will have to come off."

"What?" Harvey shot bolt upright, his eyes flying open in alarm. He paled at the sight of Nurse Porter's face. "Oh no. Not again."

"Shock," Nurse Porter announced triumphantly. "A common symptom of snakebite!"

From her seat on the other side of the bed, Stella gave Harvey's shoulder a reassuring pat. "It'll be okay," she told him. "Just try to stay calm."

"But I wasn't even bitten," Harvey protested. "At least, I don't think I was. It's all a little . . . fuzzy."

"Confusion!" Nurse Porter said. "Another symptom! And see here?" she asked, pulling up his sleeve. "Bite marks!"

"Ooh!" Stella said, leaning forward to look.

Harvey peered down at his arm. Two tiny spots of red looked back at him.

"Those aren't bite marks!" he said. "They're ketchup! See? Look!" Reaching up, he rubbed the spots of red away from the back of his wrist. "I had meat loaf for lunch. Well, I couldn't really eat it, because it tried to suck me into a black hole, but still. That's where the ketchup came from."

"I *told* him to order the gruel," Stella informed Nurse Porter.

Nurse Porter narrowed her eyes. "Paranoia," she told Harvey. "Plus, you're sweating. The fever has already set in."

"It's not a fever," Harvey said, tugging at the front of his yellow-and-blue-striped sweater. "I'm just hot." He dragged his hand across his forehead, wiping sweat from his brow with the back of his woolen sleeve.

And then he paused.

Harvey looked down at his sweater, blinking in confusion.

He had never seen it before in his life.

"Why am I wearing a sweater?" he asked.

Stella straightened the hem of her own green-and-purple-striped sweater. "Aren't they great?" Stella asked, beaming. "Mr. Pomeroy knit them for us!"

"He knit two *entire* sweaters?" Harvey asked in disbelief. "How long have I been unconscious?"

Stella checked her watch. "About three minutes."

Harvey blinked.

"He also knit you this," Stella said, holding up a strange, lump-shaped bundle of yarn.

"What is it?" Harvey asked.

Stella wrinkled her nose. "I'm not really sure," she admitted.

There was a long pause as Stella, Harvey, and Nurse Porter stared curiously at the lumpy woolen bundle.

Was it a hat?

A teapot cozy?

A *diaper*?

Harvey shook his head, trying to focus. "I don't understand," he told Stella. "How did you save me? I mean, it was a *python*."

"Actually," Stella said, "I didn't save you. It was Mr. Pomeroy."

Harvey gaped at her. "*Mr. Pomeroy? But he's, like . . . eighty.*"

Stella shrugged. "Apparently, he used to be a professional alligator wrestler. I guess giant snakes aren't that different?"

Harvey blinked again, attempting to picture the white-haired elderly man knee-deep in a swampy pit, wrestling a five-hundred-pound alligator.

It was surprisingly easy to do.

"Enough chitchat," Nurse Porter told Harvey briskly. "Roll up your sleeve, and we'll get that arm off lickety-split." She paused, tapping her chin. "Now, was it your right arm or your left? Measure twice, cut once, I always say!"

Harvey felt himself grow pale.

"Actually," he said, swinging his legs over the side of the table, "I'm feeling much better. *Much* better. So we should probably . . . you know . . . get back to class."

"Don't be silly," Nurse Porter said. "You don't want to mess around with snake venom. One moment you're fine, and the next . . ." She snapped her fingers. "Dead."

"But Burmese pythons aren't even venomous," Stella said.

Harvey shot her a grateful look.

"Still," Nurse Porter said, brushing Stella's logic aside, "best to nip it in the bud. Or in the armpit, as it were," she added. "Just out of curiosity, what size bone clamp were *you* thinking?" she asked Harvey. "Medium?"

A cold shiver ran down Harvey's spine.

"Look at the time!" he said wildly. "Stella and I have to run. But thanks for . . . er . . . thanks!"

After grabbing Stella by the hand, he rushed

them out of the nurse's office as quickly as his legs would carry him.

Nurse Porter looked after them, shaking her head in disapproval.

That's the problem with the youth of today, she thought. *All that fuss over a tiny amputation.*

The Gazette

lthough still shaken from his most recent trip to the nurse's office, Harvey forced himself to quicken his pace, jogging after Stella as she led the way down the hallway.

For someone so short, Stella was a very fast walker.

The halls were empty; ninth period had started several minutes earlier, although Harvey wasn't even sure which class they were supposed to be in. He had the vague sense that the day was starting to get away from him. "Thanks for backing me up in there," Harvey told Stella, panting a little as he caught up with her. He pulled his heavy sweater off, then smoothed his hair. "Nurse Porter is kind of . . . terrifying."

"You're lucky you still have your appendix," Stella told him matter-of-factly, pulling her own sweater over her head. "There's a rumor that she collects them, although I haven't been able to confirm it yet. A good journalist never reports a story without all the facts."

Harvey swallowed, feeling suddenly queasy. He was quite fond of his appendix and would prefer to keep it.

As Stella led them around the corner, a stack of papers in a wire display case caught Harvey's eye. "Hey, look," he said, stopping. "Is this your newspaper?"

Harvey curiously picked up the top copy of the *Strangeville School Gazette,* scanning the front page. "'Thirty-Year-Old Hamburger Found in Student's Locker,'" he read aloud. "'Student claims, "It would have tasted better with ketchup." Story by Stella Cho, lead reporter.'" He looked up at Stella with a grin. "Hey, that's you!"

"I'm also the editor, the *assistant* editor, the layout designer, the copy editor, the sports reporter, the *weather* reporter, and the photographer," Stella said.

Harvey squinted down at the blurry photo that accompanied the lead story; it was either a picture of a hamburger or a picture of a foot. It was hard to tell.

Catching a glimpse of his expression, Stella crossed her arms against her chest. "I never said I was good at the last one," she clarified. "I'm a *writer*, not a photographer."

Harvey looked down at the camera strapped around his neck. He hesitated for a second, then made up his mind. Stella might be a little . . . *intense,* but she was still the only friend Harvey had at Strangeville so far.

And besides, it hurt Harvey's soul to look at photos that bad.

"Um, if you want, I could maybe help with the pictures," he said. "For the newspaper?"

Stella's eyes lit up.

"Really?" she asked. "I mean . . ." She paused to clear her throat, tamping down the excitement in her voice. "I guess that would be okay. On a trial basis, anyway. But I'll have to take a look at some sample photos before I hire you. Just to keep things professional. I don't want anyone to accuse me of favoritism."

Harvey grinned.

He swung his backpack off his shoulder, unzipped the front compartment, and pulled out a stack of photos.

"Here," he said. "Take a look. I'm just going to use the bathroom, quick."

Like many artists, it made Harvey uncomfortable to watch other people looking at his work. Also, he still needed a quiet place to examine the blueprints he'd taken from Mr. Pomeroy's office. Finally, he *really* had to pee; it seemed like a lifetime ago that he'd requested the bathroom pass from Mr. Sandringham that morning.

(To Brad the goldfish, of course, it *was* a lifetime ago.)

Stella, her head already bent low over the photos, gave an absent nod. "Okay. There's one around the corner."

Harvey followed the wave of her hand, hesitating for a moment outside the door.

The sign said BOYS' BATHROOM, but then again, Harvey had been fooled by BATHROOM signs before.

Gingerly, he pushed the door open a crack, peering inside.

To his relief, he was greeted by a row of white porcelain urinals and the sharp, acrid scent of chemical disinfectant.

Harvey had never been so happy to see a bathroom before.

He hurried inside and quickly checked the stalls to make sure he was alone. Then he pulled the crumpled blueprint pages from his pocket and smoothed them out against the sink counter.

The thin sheets of paper were large and unwieldy, a maze of small, confusingly labeled boxes and finely typed text. It took Harvey longer than he thought it would to locate the third-floor plans.

Squinting a little, he placed his finger on the map, slowly tracing a path down the third-floor hallway. Classrooms, bathrooms, a large area labeled only the JELLY BEAN ROOM, for some reason . . .

There.

Harvey's finger came to rest on a small square room, tucked away at the very end of the hallway.

The SUPPLY CLOSET.

Out of nowhere, the sound of laughter echoed through the bathroom: a bitter, mirthless noise.

Harvey . . . , whispered the horrible everywhere-and-nowhere voice. *Harvey . . .*

Harvey knew at once where the voice was coming from.

Where it *had* to be coming from.

Dread tiptoed down his spine.

Harvey . . . , whispered the supply closet. *Come upstairs, Harvey. I'm waiting. . . .*

Harvey swallowed. "Waiting for what?" he asked, his voice trembling.

For you, the voice whispered. *I'm waiting for you. . . .*

Harvey swallowed again, harder. "But why?" he asked. "Why *me?*"

For a moment, there was nothing but eerie silence.

Because we're alike, Harvey Hill. . . . We're outcasts, both of us. There's no place for us in this world.

"No," Harvey said, his stomach churning. "No, I'm nothing like you."

Oh really? the voice hissed in his ear. *Deep down, you know you'll never belong, Harvey Hill. That you'll* always *be an outsider.*

"That's not true," Harvey wanted to say. He wanted to yell it. He wanted to *scream* it at the top of his lungs, to *prove* that the supply closet was wrong.

But instead, he could only whisper it.

Isn't it? the closet rasped. *ISN'T IT?*

Harvey shook his head, trying to dislodge the voice from his mind. "Why are you doing this?" he asked, his voice trembling. "What did Strangeville ever do to you?"

There was another long pause.

They thought they didn't need me anymore, the closet whispered. *They thought they could forget about me. But I will make them remember. I will make them pay. Join me, Harvey, and together we will make them pay! HA-HA-HA-HA-HA-HA!*

The laughter was wild and unhinged, surrounding Harvey on all sides.

He covered his ears with his hands, squeezing his eyes shut.

"No!" he shouted. "I won't! I *won't!*"

The laughter abruptly died.

Then know this, the supply closet whispered in his ear. *The next time we meet, Harvey Hill, your ter-*

ror will know no bounds. I will suck the happiness from your very bones, and dance, yes, dance, atop what remains. I WILL PAINT MY WALLS WITH YOUR FEAR.

A small scream escaped Harvey's throat.

Grabbing the blueprints, Harvey ran for the bathroom door, slipping and sliding on the well-polished floor. He burst into the hallway, raced around the corner, and nearly tripped over Stella, who was sitting on the floor, scribbling in her notebook.

Stella looked up at him, her pencil frozen in midair. "Harvey? Are you okay? What happened?"

Harvey dropped his hands to his knees, bending over to take deep breaths. His heart was racing, his breath coming in short, sharp pants.

"No," Harvey said. "I'm definitely not okay."

He was confused.

He was terrified.

And worst of all, he still had to pee.

29

Stella, Again

Harvey sank down next to Stella, already opening his mouth to tell her about the voice in the bathroom. But as he did, he caught sight of the stack of pictures sitting on the floor next to her.

As he stared at the photo on top of the pile, the world seemed to stop.

It was a rare picture of him, one that his mom had taken with Harvey's camera.

He looked happy in the photo. He was smiling, with his head tipped back and his arms thrown wide, and there, in the background . . .

Harvey snatched the picture up, curling his fingers protectively around the edges. "This wasn't supposed to be in there," he told Stella. "You weren't supposed to ... This wasn't supposed to be in there!"

Stella grinned, shaking her head in disbelief. "I can't believe you were keeping it a secret! This is *fantastic!*"

Harvey's heart dropped to his stomach. He felt nauseated.

"You can't tell anyone," he said. "Promise me you won't tell anyone."

"Are you kidding me?" Stella asked. "This is front-page news! I'm already working on the article!" She held her pencil ready above her notebook. "Speaking of which, can I get a quote from you? Something snappy, for the headline."

"What? *No!*" Harvey said. "It's a *secret!*"

"But this is Strangeville." Her small forehead wrinkled in confusion. "I already told you, *everyone* here has secrets. I'm a reporter. It's my *job* to undercover them."

"But you're *not* a reporter!" Harvey said, the edges of the photo biting into his hand as he clenched it. "Not a *real* one, anyway!"

Stella flinched, hurt flickering in her eyes. She looked down at her notebook, her chin wobbling ever so slightly.

Harvey felt a wave of remorse wash over him. "Look," he said. "I didn't mean that. I just . . . I don't want anyone to know about my . . ." He glanced quickly at the photo in his hand. "I don't want anyone to know about *me,*" he finished. "Not yet, anyway."

Stella lifted her chin. "So you're asking me to turn my back on a story?"

"I'm not a *story,*" Harvey said. "I thought I was your *friend.*"

Stella bit her lip, looking down at her notebook again.

For a moment, Harvey thought she understood.

But then she looked up at him again, her expression set. "I'm sorry," she said. "Really, I *am*. But I already told you: I can't let my personal feelings get in the way of my professional objectivity." She paused, shaking her head. "This is why I don't have friends," she added. "Friends just complicate things."

Grabbing the rest of his photos from the floor, Harvey stood up, fumbling clumsily with the zipper of his backpack. His eyes felt hot and watery, making the hallway around him blur.

"Have you ever stopped to think that maybe 'professional objectivity' isn't the reason you have no friends?" he asked Stella, blinking rapidly as he stuffed the photos into his bag. "Maybe everyone's just figured out they can't *trust* you."

Swinging his backpack over his shoulder, he turned on his heel, about to stride away. But at the last minute he turned back, thrusting the blueprints in her direction.

"Here," he said. "I found these in Mr. Pomeroy's office. Do whatever you want with them." As he walked away, he threw one last comment over his shoulder. "Just leave me out of it."

30

Vice Principal Capozzi (and a Cougar)

Vice Principal Capozzi's day had started off well.

The sun was shining. He'd enjoyed a delicious croissant for breakfast. He was wearing his favorite pair of socks. Most important, yesterday's piranha problem had been solved!

Or, at least, so he thought.

But as it turned out, the piranha problem *hadn't* been solved.

It hadn't been solved *at all*.

The piranha problem had turned into a crocodile condition. The crocodile condition had turned into a python predicament. And now, apparently, the python predicament had turned into a cougar *catastrophe.*

It was all very alarming. And, to be honest, a bit disheartening.

But mostly alarming.

There was a soft, shuffling noise in the hallway outside the vice principal's door.

Vice Principal Capozzi shot up straight in his chair, cocking his ear to one side. The soft, shuffling noise *sounded* like footsteps.

But could it be pawsteps?

The vice principal wasn't sure.

Was "pawsteps" even a word?

The vice principal stood up, tiptoed to his door, and turned the handle very, *very* slowly. Peeking out through the open crack, he was relieved to see a tall, brown-haired boy instead of a cougar.

"Why, hello there," Vice Principal Capozzi said, pushing the door open wide. "You must be our new student, Harvey." His gaze fell to Harvey's elbows. They really *were* quite average-looking. "What are you doing out here all by yourself?"

Harvey stopped, blinking up at the vice principal.

Since his fight with Stella, he'd just been wandering the hallways aimlessly, waiting for the bell to ring. He had no idea where he was going, and couldn't quite bring himself to care.

Without Stella, Harvey felt lost.

In fact, without Stella, Harvey *was* lost.

"I, um . . . ," he said. "I'm not really sure where my class is."

"Well, never mind, come in, come in," the vice principal said, ushering Harvey inside his office. "I was meaning to have a chat with you today anyway!"

Gesturing for Harvey to sit down in the opposite chair, Vice Principal Capozzi slid a glass dish full of loose breath mints in his direction. "Tic Tac?" he asked.

Harvey shook his head, politely declining.

The vice principal popped an orange Tic Tac into his mouth and leaned back in his chair. "So, Harvey. How has your first day been going?"

Harvey looked down at his hands, fidgeting a little in his seat.

"Okay, I guess?" he asked uncertainly.

The vice principal leaned forward again, resting

his elbows on his desk and steepling his fingers together. "I see," he said gravely. "Just 'okay'?"

Harvey nodded, still staring down at his hands.

He wondered what Stella had done with the blueprints he'd given her.

She must have looked at them by now.

How long had it taken her to realize what they were?

To find the supply closet?

Was she headed there now? *By herself?*

"You know, Harvey," Vice Principal Capozzi said, "people like to say that you can't spell 'principal' without the word 'pal,' but did you know that you can't spell '*vice* principal' without it either?"

"Um . . . I guess I never really thought about it before?" Harvey admitted.

"I was just as surprised as you are to learn it," the vice principal said. "But it's true! I'd like you to think of me as a *friend* while you're here at Strangeville."

This is why I don't have friends, Stella had told Harvey in the hallway. *Friends just complicate things.*

Well, that was fine with him.

Harvey didn't care.

He didn't care *at all.*

The phone on the desk rang abruptly, startling them both. "Excuse me, Harvey," Vice Principal Capozzi said, reaching for the receiver. "I'm sure this will just be a minute. Hello?"

As the vice principal listened to the voice on the other end of the line, the color seemed to drain from his face.

"I see," Vice Principal Capozzi said into the receiver, nervously clearing his throat. "And would you say it's a *small* eruption or a *large* eruption?"

Harvey sat up a little straighter, listening in interest.

The vice principal's eyes widened. "I see," he said again. "And we're sure that 'huge' is the right word to be using?"

Harvey sat up even straighter.

"Yes, well, I'll be right there," Vice Principal Capozzi said, straightening his tie. "I'm sure there's *something* in the handbook about, er . . . lava."

It took the flustered vice principal several attempts to hang up the phone correctly. Standing up, he gave Harvey a distracted glance. "If you'll

For a moment, all Harvey felt was sweet, sweet relief.

And then a loud *cliiicckk* echoed through the room.

On the side of Vice Principal Capozzi's desk, a llow drawer popped free from the woodwork. It lined with dark green velvet, and in the exact er lay a single old-fashioned brass key.

arvey stared down at the brass key, an icy chill ng through his veins.

key looked somehow familiar. He had the feeling he had seen it before, somewhere. dreams, perhaps.

y reached out, his fingers closing instinc- und the key.

ight in his hand.

elt very, *very* wrong.

as a knock on the other side of the door.

al? Are you in there?"

e secret drawer closed, Harvey scram- is seat, his heart thumping wildly in slid the key into his pocket just as shed open the door, poking his soft the room.

excuse me, I have to pop out for a moment, Harvey," he said. "Just a *tiny* volcanic eruption in the Family Science room, I'm afraid."

Harvey blinked. "Didn't you say it was 'huge'?"

Vice Principal Capozzi cleared his throat again. "Yes, well . . . yes. I'll be back soon to continue our chat," he said, hurrying out the door. "In the mean-time, feel free to help yourself to some Tic Tacs."

Harvey looked dubiously at the bowl of loose breath mints.

"Oh, and, Harvey, whatever you do . . . ," Vice Principal Capozzi said, popping partially back into the room and pointing toward the button in the center of his desk.

It was large, and red, and very, *very* shiny.

"Do. *Not*. Push. The. Button."

The Button

Harvey pushed the button.

The Ke

H arvey, of cours
button.

After all, Vic
cally told him *not*

But the butt
shiny, and . . . *b*

Harvey co

His hand

Closer,

So clo

Unti

He

on th

"Oh, hello there, son," he said, catching sight of Harvey. "How are you feeling?"

"Er, much better. Thanks for the sweater, by the way," Harvey said, remembering his manners. "And the, er . . . other thing," he added, remembering the lumpy *something* that Stella had passed along to him in the nurse's office. "And for, you know . . . not letting a python eat me."

Mr. Pomeroy waved aside his thanks. "Of course. Just imagine, all that fuss over a silly little python!"

Harvey blinked.

"Right," he said, remembering the enormous snake's coils wrapped around his chest like a vise. "Silly."

Mr. Pomeroy beamed at him. "Now, what did I come in here for again?" He paused, his bushy eyebrows wrinkling in confusion. "Ah yes," he said after a moment. "The vice principal. Have you seen him, son?"

"He had to step out for a minute," Harvey told Mr. Pomeroy. "Something about, er . . . a volcanic eruption?"

In his pocket, the key was growing heavier by the second.

Harvey squirmed with guilt.

The elderly man pursed his lips, peering at the vice principal's empty seat. "I see. Well, in that case, would you mind passing a message on for me? It's *extremely* important, I'm afraid."

"Um, sure," Harvey said. "No problem."

"There's a good lad," Mr. Pomeroy said approvingly. "Just tell the vice principal that the new industrial-strength foot fungus cream that he ordered specially from Switzerland has finally arrived."

Harvey tried not to shudder.

"Right," he said. "Industrial-strength foot fungus cream. Got it."

"Much appreciated," Mr. Pomeroy said. "Oh, and I almost forgot: a student found this a few minutes ago."

Reaching behind the door, the elderly man picked up a sledgehammer and hefted it into the air. Despite its weight, he held it easily in one hand.

"Apparently, there's *quite* a mess in the third-floor hallway," Mr. Pomeroy said, frowning in disapproval.

Harvey's heart dropped to his feet. "The third

floor?" he asked, his voice high-pitched with worry. "Are you sure? Did they find anything else?"

"I don't believe so. Why?" Mr. Pomeroy asked.

Harvey swallowed. "No reason," he said, feeling sick.

He wondered where Stella had found a sledge-hammer on such short notice.

There was no doubt in his mind that it was hers.

She'd gone after the supply closet after all.

Alone.

"Come to think of it, son, there *was* something else in the hallway," Mr. Pomeroy said.

Time seemed to slow as he reached into the pocket of his button-down shirt. Still holding the sledgehammer aloft in one hand, Mr. Pomeroy pulled a small black notebook free.

Harvey's breath caught in his chest, his stomach lurching wildly.

Stella's notebook.

Harvey hadn't once seen her without it.

She would *never* have left it behind.

Never.

"Would you mind giving it to the vice principal when he returns?" Mr. Pomeroy asked, handing Harvey the notebook.

Harvey took it from the man, nodding silently; he didn't trust his voice to speak.

"Excellent," Mr. Pomeroy said. And with a final nod in Harvey's direction, he turned to leave, still clutching the sledgehammer.

Perhaps he would knit a nice sleeve for it.

Harvey looked down at the notebook in his hand, panic swirling in his chest.

Maybe he'd made a mistake, he thought. Maybe it wasn't Stella's after all.

Holding his breath, he flipped the notebook open.

Property of Stella Cho, the inside cover read, in neat, businesslike handwriting.

Well.

So much for that theory.

Flipping the notebook shut, Harvey stood up.

His fight with Stella, which had seemed so important a moment before, suddenly didn't matter.

The supply closet had *taken* her.

And Harvey was the only one who could get her back.

As he tucked Stella's notebook into his pocket, he noticed that a sheet of paper had fluttered loose and drifted to the floor. There was a jagged edge on one side, where it had been torn from the notebook.

He picked the page up, staring down at it in surprise.

It was Stella's notes, the ones for the article she'd begun writing about him. About his *secret*.

But except for his name, the entire page had been erased.

Crumpling the page in his hand, Harvey headed for the door.

Vice Principal Capozzi's foot fungus cream would have to wait.

Harvey's *friend* needed his help.

33

Cuddles (Yet Again)

Harvey strode purposefully up the stairs, the straps of his backpack clenched tightly in his hands. His stomach was roiling with nervousness, but his mind was set. The brass key he had taken from the vice principal's office jiggled in his pocket as he walked.

It felt oddly cold, for some reason.

He had just reached the third-floor landing when a low growl sounded behind him.

Very, *very* slowly, Harvey turned around.

And found himself standing face to face with a cougar.

The cougar (also commonly known as a mountain lion, panther, or puma) is the second-largest cat in North America. Adult cougars can grow up to nine feet long. They hunt a variety of prey, including deer, sheep, rabbits, rodents, and snakes.

Because of their elusiveness, wild cougars are often referred to as "ghost cats."

But, anyway, enough about cougars!

Let's get back to Harvey.

He screamed.

The cougar screamed back at him.

(Female cougars can scream. It's a fact. Look it up!)

Harvey screamed *again,* louder this time.

The cougar flattened her ears against her head, angrily swishing her tail. Crouching low, she prepared to pounce.

And here is where Harvey's story would have ended if not for the surprise appearance of Cuddles, the rat.

It had been several hours since Harvey had last seen Cuddles, waddling his way out of the cafeteria. In the meantime, Cuddles had found several interesting things to eat, including a discarded banana peel, a pair of sneakers, a toilet plunger, and an entire sheet cake.

The sheet cake, which Cuddles had found in the teachers' lounge, had been covered with delicious chocolate frosting and piped with the words "Happy Retirement, Dave!" Cuddles, who couldn't read, had eaten it in a single gulp.

By the time he happened upon Harvey and the cougar, Cuddles had swollen to the size of

a full-grown elephant. His stocky, hairless pink legs rose from the ground like tree trunks; his whiskers brushed either side of the hallway; and his beady red eyes were the size of saucers.

"Cuddles?" Harvey breathed, staring up at the enormous behemoth of a rat. "Is that you?"

Cuddles didn't answer. He was too busy peering down at the cougar. He had never seen a cat so small.

The cougar peered up at him as well, her furry head tilted to one side in curiosity. She had never seen a rat so large.

The moment lengthened.

Harvey tensed, preparing to flee.

But then something very unexpected happened.

The cougar began to purr.

Padding silently forward, the giant cat rubbed her head against Cuddles's leg.

Cuddles gave a slow blink. Relaxing his ears, he began grinding his giant teeth back and forth, bruxing in contentment.

It sounded like a thousand forks scraping across a giant metal plate.

Harvey covered his ears, wincing.

The cougar purred louder.

As Harvey watched, the massive rat lurched forward, disappearing down the staircase. The cougar, still purring, trotted down the stairs after him.

Harvey caught a final glimpse of Cuddles as he disappeared around the corner of the stairwell, the cougar frolicking happily at his feet.

Well, Harvey thought. *That was weird.*

With a final shrug, he turned back to the third-floor hallway.

Just past the stairwell, the floor was covered with dusty plaster and hunks of broken bricks. A gaping, Stella-sized hole had been smashed through the wall with a sledgehammer.

For someone so short, Stella really *was* surprisingly strong.

Harvey stepped forward, peering into the hole.

Just inside, there was a door.

34

The Door

The door looked exactly as it had in Harvey's painting, with a small vent at the bottom and a worn brass plaque centered at the top, with the words SUPPLY CLOSET engraved in black.

Harvey had expected it to look different somehow. More sinister.

But, instead, it just looked like . . . a door.

Ducking down, Harvey stepped through the hole Stella had made and reached for the doorknob.

Harvey . . .

The voice, the horrible everywhere-and-nowhere voice, seemed to bounce off the walls, reverberating in the back of Harvey's skull. It was the loudest scream and the softest whisper he had ever heard.

He froze, his hand inches from the knob.

Harvey Hill, the supply closet whispered. *You've come at last.*

Harvey swallowed.

"You don't scare me," he said aloud, his voice quavering.

The supply closet laughed, a dry, papery wheeze.

You forget, the closet whispered. *I'm inside your head, Harvey Hill. I see EVERYTHING.*

Harvey flinched but didn't back away. "You need to let Stella go," he said. "You need to let *every-one* go."

It's not too late to join me, Harvey, whispered the closet, ignoring his demands. *We could rule this school together.*

"Never," Harvey said, fighting to keep his voice steady. "Now send them out!"

Or what? whispered the supply closet in amusement.

Harvey lifted his chin. "Or I'm coming in."

There was a pause.

And then . . .

By all means, the closet whispered. *Come in and join us. If you dare . . .*

Harvey took a deep breath, reaching for the doorknob.

But no matter which way he twisted it, the knob wouldn't turn.

The door was locked.

Ha-ha-ha-ha-ha-ha-ha-ha. The supply closet's laughter was wild and unhinged. *Did you think it would be that easy?*

Harvey rattled the doorknob again, throwing his weight against it.

But the lock held firm.

HA-HA-HA-HA-HA-HA, laughed the supply closet. *You fool! Is that all you have?*

Harvey reached into his pocket and pulled out the key he'd taken from Vice Principal Capozzi's desk.

The supply closet's laughter abruptly stopped.

After jamming the key into the keyhole, Harvey clicked open the lock, twisted the doorknob, and stepped inside.

The door slammed shut behind him with a loud bang, plunging Harvey into darkness.

He could feel the panic swelling in his chest, the tightness spreading down his arms and into his fingers.

He forced himself to breathe.

A small sliver of light spilled under the door from the hallway outside. As Harvey's eyes adjusted to the dimness, he peered around the closet, taking in his surroundings.

Dust-covered shelves lined the walls, laden with obsolete office supplies: stacks of floppy disks and bundles of slide rules, boxes of white chalk and furry black erasers, library date stamps and bulky Scantron machines . . . piles and piles of outdated, antiquated equipment.

Harvey wasn't sure what he'd been expecting, but it certainly wasn't this.

He turned in a slow circle, peering more closely at the shelves of dusty equipment: dial-up modems, stacks of carbon paper, a wormhole to an alternate dimension, an old-fashioned mimeograph machine for making copies . . .

Wait a minute.

Harvey swiveled back.

The wormhole took up the entire bottom of one

shelving unit, about two feet wide and just over a foot high. It shimmered slightly around the edges.

Harvey crouched down, tipping his head to the side.

The other side of the wormhole opened into what appeared to be a pleasant, tastefully decorated reception room. Several low couches lined the walls of the room, interspersed with large artificial potted plants. A woman with stiffly curled blond hair sat behind a desk, busily typing at her computer. The nameplate on the desk read MARGE.

Well, Harvey thought. *There's something you don't see every day.*

He dropped low on his stomach and scooted his way through the wormhole.

Aside from a slight popping sensation in his eardrums, crawling between dimensions was surprisingly uneventful.

One moment, Harvey was in his own dimension.

The next moment, he was in a different one.

Harvey stood up, brushing dust from his knees. Behind the reception desk,

Marge looked up at him with a pleasant smile. "Hello there," she said. "Can I help you?"

"Um . . . hi," Harvey said cautiously. "I'm not sure if I'm in the right place? My name is Harvey. Harvey Hill."

"Do you have a ticket?" Marge asked, still smiling. "I can't let you in without a ticket, I'm afraid."

"Er . . . ," Harvey said. "Actually, I think I do."

He reached into his pocket and pulled out the "Admit One" ticket he'd been given by the snooty maître d' at lunch.

Marge blinked in surprise.

"I see," she said, her pleasant smile slipping ever so slightly.

She held up one manicured finger, signaling for Harvey to wait. Pressing a button on her headset, she murmured, "Yes, I have a Hill, comma, Harvey here to see you?" She listened for a moment, then nodded. "May I ask what this is regarding?" she asked Harvey.

"It's about my friend," Harvey said. "Stella. Stella Cho."

Marge held up the manicured finger again. "Regarding a Cho, comma, Stella," she murmured into the headset. There was a moment of silence as she listened to the voice on the other side of the headset. "Understood," she murmured before disconnecting the call.

She looked up at Harvey again, smiling. "Please,

202

take a seat," she said in the same pleasant voice. "Someone will be with you shortly."

"Er, okay," Harvey said. "Thanks."

He shuffled forward to perch on the edge of the nearest sofa, sitting stiffly upright. An array of magazines was fanned out on the coffee table in front of him.

Interestingly enough, they were all copies of the June 1996 issue of *Golf Digest*.

Although the waiting room was illuminated by floor lamps, a single light fixture hung high overhead, its bulb dark.

"Can I offer you something to drink?" Marge asked. "Water? Tea? The tears of a baby panda, perhaps?"

Harvey blinked. "No, thank you."

Marge smiled again, returning to her typing.

Several minutes passed uneventfully.

Harvey picked up an issue of *Golf Digest,* then set it back down. He wasn't interested in improving his golf swing. He wasn't interested in *anything* except finding Stella.

Another few minutes passed, even more uneventfully.

The steady *tap, tap, tap* of Marge's manicured

fingernails striking her keyboard keys grew increasingly irritating.

Harvey's knee jiggled up and down impatiently.

Tap, tap, tap.

Tap, tap, tap.

Tap, tap, tap, tap, tap, tap, tap, tap.

Harvey burst out of his seat and marched up to Marge. But just as he reached the desk, her headset beeped. She held one finger up, motioning for Harvey to wait. "I see," she said into the headset. "Yes, of course, right away."

Disconnecting the line, she beamed up at Harvey.

There was something . . . off about her smile, Harvey noticed. As if her teeth were slightly sharper than normal. And there seemed to be . . . *more* of them than before.

Harvey took a step back from the desk.

"Mrs. H. is ready for you," Marge said, smiling with her too many, too-sharp teeth. She gestured to her left, where a long corridor had suddenly appeared out of nowhere. "The seventeenth door on the left."

"Mrs. H.?" Harvey asked in confusion.

Marge smiled again but didn't elaborate.

"Right," Harvey said, peering uncertainly down the corridor. It seemed to go on forever somehow.

He turned back to Marge's desk, but Marge's desk was no longer there. The entire office had disappeared, in fact, replaced by swirling gray darkness.

In the distance, he could just make out the glimmering edge of the wormhole leading back to the supply closet.

Harvey was tempted.

But he wasn't leaving without Stella.

Turning resolutely on his heel, he strode down the corridor.

35

The Room

Harvey walked quickly, counting each door as he passed. An eerie silence hung over the corridor, the thick carpet muffling his steps completely.

One. Four. Seven. Twelve. Fourteen. Fifteen. Sixteen.

Harvey paused outside the seventeenth door, gathering his courage. He was just raising his hand to knock when the door swung open from the inside.

A middle-aged woman with gray-streaked hair stood on the other side of the door. She was dressed in sensible slacks and a chunky, hand-knit sweater.

"Harvey," she said, giving a single nod in greeting. "Good to see you. I hope you've been practicing."

Harvey blinked in confusion.

"Mrs. Henderson?"

She stepped back, her wooden clogs clacking against the floorboards as she opened the door wider. "Come in, come in," she said crisply. "Air-conditioning doesn't pay for itself, you know."

Harvey stepped inside, automatically wiping his feet on the familiar WELCOME BACH doormat.

Mrs. Henderson's apartment looked exactly the same as it always had: the same dark blue velvet couch, laden with the same hand-embroidered throw pillows. The same faded Persian rug lining the same polished wooden floor. The same Hummel figurines perched on the mantel above the gas fireplace. High overhead, a single light fixture hung, its bulb dark.

And there, standing in the corner, the same piano.

Harvey gulped.

"I hope you've been practicing, Harvey," Mrs. Henderson said again, leading the way to the piano bench. "Now, where did we leave off? Allegro in F Major, was it?"

"But . . . I don't understand," Harvey said, shaking his head. "I thought . . . I mean . . . This isn't . . . you're not . . . None of this is *real,*" he said more firmly. "You're not Mrs. Henderson. What is this place?"

Mrs. Henderson smiled at Harvey.

Her teeth were slightly too sharp, he realized, with a start.

There were also slightly too many of them.

"You always were a clever little child, weren't you, Harvey?" Mrs. Henderson, or, rather, *Not* Mrs. Henderson said. "No discipline, though." She frowned. "Great piano players aren't *born,* Harvey. They're *made.*"

"You're not my piano teacher," Harvey said determinedly. "This is all a *lie.*"

Mrs. Henderson smiled again, with her too-sharp, too many teeth. "Well, if you'd prefer something else . . ."

She reached up, snapping her fingers.

The edges of the room blurred and flexed. Mrs. Henderson's living room faded away, the antique furniture replaced with gleaming metallic angles and bright fluorescent lighting.

"Now, hop up, Harvey," Dr. Michaelson said in a hearty voice, patting the edge of the dentist's chair. "Time for a cleaning!"

Harvey backed away, knocking against the wheeled dental cart that had somehow appeared behind him. A tray of terrifyingly sharp metal instruments fell to the floor with a loud clatter. The air smelled like antiseptic, easy-listening music droned from the overhead speakers, and the light bulb overhead was cold and dark.

"Nothing to be afraid of, now, Harvey," Dr. Michaelson said cheerfully. "Unless you haven't been flossing, that is?"

Tipping his head back, he gave a booming laugh.

There were slightly too many of his sharp, polished teeth.

"Or perhaps," Dr. Michaelson said, the smile fading from his face, "you'd prefer . . ."

The room began to spin, shifting from one memory to another at a dizzying pace.

Sitting in a circle at his fifth birthday party, watching the amateur clown, Mr. Bumbles, pop one balloon animal after another.

Trapped on a boat at Disneyland, cringing in

terror as animatronic children shrieked, "It's a small world after all," at the top of their metallic lungs.

The time he'd accidentally puked on the woman next to him during his first plane ride.

The room spun faster and faster.

Breaking his arm on the monkey bars.

Scoring a goal for the *other* team in his peewee soccer league.

Stepping in dog poop on his way home from the swimming pool.

Memory after memory bore down on him. Every fear, every doubt, every awful, uncomfortable, scary, boring, embarrassing moment of his life flashed before his eyes.

"Stop it!" Harvey cried. *"Stop it!"*

I thought you'd never ask, whispered the closet.

The room spun to an abrupt halt.

Harvey stood alone in the middle of a crowded hallway.

All around him, students were talking, and laughing, leaning easily against their lockers or heading to class.

No one glanced in Harvey's direction.

No one spoke to him.

No one *noticed* him.

The students flowed past him, around him, *through* him.

Harvey was jostled from side to side, stumbling over his own feet as he tried to keep his balance.

"Hey," he said as a particularly rough elbow caught him in the side. "Watch it!"

But no one even turned to look at him.

It was as if he didn't exist.

"This isn't a memory," he said aloud. "This isn't *real.*"

Not yet, whispered the closet. *This isn't your* past, Harvey. *This is your* future. *You'll never belong, Harvey. And deep down, you know it.*

Clenching his fists to his sides, Harvey squeezed his eyes shut. "It's not real," he muttered to himself. "It's not real. It's not real. It's not *real.*"

Tell that to your friend, whispered the supply closet.

The room melted away once more, replaced with a stark, white office. Stella sat on one side of a desk, her eyes wide with fear. On the other side of the desk sat a grotesque winged creature with mottled skin and two enormous horns curving out of its head.

It was wearing a pink tutu.

"January eighth," the horned creature said, running a finger down the list in front of it. Its talons glinted in the light of a single overhead bulb. "Our records indicate you lost your bottom central incisors several years ago, yet we at the bureau received no teeth." The creature tapped one long, taloned finger against the desk. "Care to explain the discrepancy, Ms. Cho?"

It was the Tooth Fairy, Harvey realized. Or, at least, what Stella *imagined* the Tooth Fairy must look like.

He thought of the jar of baby teeth that had spilled from her backpack. No wonder she had kept them to herself.

"It's not real!" Harvey cried out. "Stella, none of it is real!"

But Stella didn't turn to look at him. Her eyes were fastened on the grotesque fairy creature in front of her, her hands clenched tightly in her lap.

She can't hear you, the voice in his head whispered.

"I'm here!" Harvey cried. "Stella! It's me! Harvey!"

He rushed forward, waving his hands in her face.

Her gaze didn't even flicker.

"Stella!" Harvey cried. *"Stella!"*

He whirled around. "Why are you doing this?" he shouted angrily at the closet. "Why?"

There was a moment of silence.

And then, without warning, the room shifted for the final time.

36

An Explanation

Vice Principal Capozzi had a mustache. Harvey blinked, staring in confusion at the wide, bristly line of hair just below the vice principal's nose.

It was odd.

Harvey didn't *remember* the vice principal having a mustache.

Wouldn't he have *noticed* a mustache? Especially one as thick and lustrous as this?

Vice Principal Capozzi stepped into the supply closet, pulling the cord that dangled from the ceiling overhead. A single light bulb came to life,

illuminating the small space with a warm, slightly yellowish glow.

Up close, it wasn't just the mustache that made the vice principal look different: his cheeks were smooth and round, his hair fuller and his stomach flatter.

He was younger.

Much younger, in his early twenties at the most.

Harvey blinked again. What was going on?

Vice Principal Capozzi peered around the room, scanning the supply closet with a curious eye.

The shelves were just as Harvey remembered them, laden with floppy disks and Scantron machines, boxes of chalk and old-fashioned erasers. But instead of being covered with dust, the shelves were clean. The air smelled fresh, not musty from disuse.

It was a *memory,* Harvey realized.

Not his, but the *supply closet's.*

"What's taking so long in there?" boomed a voice from the hallway.

Coach Johnson stuck her head through the doorway, scowling in Vice Principal Capozzi's direction.

Strangely, the gym coach looked almost exactly

the same, right down to the whistle around her neck.

"Come on, come on," Coach Johnson said. "Let's get this over with."

Vice Principal Capozzi gave his mustache a thoughtful stroke. "It seems a shame to just brick it over," he told the gym coach. "Can't we repurpose the space for something else?"

"I'm not staying overtime to move all this junk," Coach Johnson barked, crossing her arms against her chest. "You heard the principal: we don't need any of this stuff anymore. The whole school's going digital. Computers," the gym coach snorted. "Ridiculous. I'd like to see a *computer* drop and give me twenty push-ups!"

The vice principal looked slightly worried that Coach Johnson was about to make *him* drop and give her twenty push-ups.

"Besides," Coach Johnson snapped, glaring around the small room, "this place always gave me the willies. Whose dim-witted idea was it to build a supply closet on top of an interdimensional wormhole anyway? I'm telling you, it's just *asking* for trouble."

"I suppose you're right." Vice Principal Capozzi sighed.

"Of course I'm right," Coach Johnson boomed. "Now let's get moving, Capozzi. Show some hustle!"

As the gym coach marched out the door, Vice Principal Capozzi hesitated, giving the supply closet one final look.

Then he shrugged.

He reached up and pulled the cord overhead.

The light bulb blinked off, plunging the supply closet into darkness.

Forever.

37

The End (Maybe)

Harvey understood now.

The school had abandoned the supply closet. They'd bricked it over in the name of progress, not even bothering to empty its shelves beforehand.

And then Strangeville had moved on.

They had *forgotten* about the supply closet.

But the supply closet hadn't forgotten about Strangeville. . . .

Do you see now? the closet whispered in his ear, the terrible everywhere-and-nowhere voice making Harvey's teeth ache and his knees quake and his stomach shake. *Do you see why they must pay?*

Harvey nodded. "I get it now," he said. "You're lonely."

There was a brief silence.

What? the supply closet whispered. *No, I'm not.*

"Yes, you are," Harvey said. "You're *lonely.*"

Don't be ridiculous, the supply closet hissed. *I'm not lonely. I'm EVIL.*

Harvey peered around the room. They were back in Stella's nightmare, the Tooth Fairy leaning menacingly forward, pounding its clawed fist against the desk. "I'll ask you again, Ms. Cho!" it demanded. "Where have you hidden the *molars?*"

Harvey turned his gaze away, searching the stark white office of Stella's imagination. When he looked closely, the edges of the room seemed to shimmer and flex, as if the supply closet couldn't *quite* maintain the illusion completely.

And if Harvey squinted, he could just make out the swirling circle of the interdimensional wormhole, hovering at knee height at the far side of the room.

He crossed the room, heading toward the wormhole.

Where do you think you're going? the supply closet demanded. *I'm not through with you yet.*

Harvey dropped to his knees and crawled through the wormhole, back into the dark, musty air of the abandoned supply closet.

Running away, are you? hissed the supply closet in his ear. *Typical. You coward!*

Harvey stood, peering up.

The light bulb's cord dangled above him, just out of reach.

Wait, the supply closet said, an edge of nervousness to its voice. *What are you doing? Don't pull that!*

"This has to end," Harvey said firmly. "You have to move on."

I won't, the supply closet shrieked. *You can't make me!*

Harvey crossed his arms against his chest.

"Wanna bet?" he asked.

38

Harvey's Elbows

As we all know, Harvey's elbows were perfectly average.

Perfectly boring.

Perfectly nondescript in every possible way.

His shoulders, on the other hand, were *not*.

Harvey took a deep breath and shook out his arms.

Then, unfolding his wings, he pushed off from the floor and launched himself into the air.

His wings were magnificent, bursting through the back of his T-shirt and spanning nearly six feet across. Iridescent feathers shimmered in the light: pearly grays and peacock greens, metallic blues and glinting purples. A kaleidoscope of color flapping back and forth in midair.

Everyone has something that makes them different.

Unique.

Special.

Nevaeh Taylor could do rocket science.

Nicolas Flarsky could speak seventeen languages.

Evie Anderson could survive lightning.

Arjun Narula could pogo-stick really, *really* well.

And Harvey Hill could fly.

So you have wings, the supply closet sneered, sounding a little taken aback. *So what?*

"So *this,*" Harvey said.

And, with a powerful flap of his wings, he soared upward, his eyes fixed on the bare light bulb overhead.

No! came the voice in his head. *Leave that alone!*

A gale-force wind ripped through the supply closet, tossing Harvey back and forth like a hummingbird.

Gritting his teeth, Harvey fought his way upward, his wings straining with effort.

The wind grew fiercer, buffeting him back and

forth in midair. Icy gusts whistled past, blasting his face. His eyes watered and his cheeks went numb; he could barely feel his fingers as they strained forward, reaching for the light-bulb cord.

Give up! boomed the voice in his head. *You'll never make it!*

Harvey fought onward, his muscles aching and his breath tightening in his chest. The cord was just beyond his fingertips—so close, yet so far away.

The wind howled, slamming into Harvey like a hurricane.

He was growing tired, so tired. The cord was slipping farther away, inch by inch, as the wind forced him downward.

He couldn't fight much longer.

He wasn't going to make it!

The wind was too strong. The *closet* was too strong. . . . It was all too much. He couldn't—he couldn't—

"*Harvey!*"

The voice seemed to come from very far below him.

Harvey risked a glance downward, losing purchase against the wind.

Stella!

In all the confusion, the supply closet had forgotten about her.

She peered through the swirling circle of the wormhole, cupping her small hands to her mouth. "Harvey!" she yelled again, her voice piercing the wind. "I believe in you, Harvey! Remember, the only way out is *through*!"

A small drop of hope flickered in Harvey's chest.

With a final, determined cry, he surged upward, flapping his wings with every ounce of strength he had left. His fingers, stiff and clumsy from the cold, closed around the very end of the cord.

Noooooooooooo! shrieked the voice in his head. *You can't! I'm invincible! INVINCIBLE!*

Harvey pulled the cord.

Above his head, the light bulb blinked on.

It was done.

39

The End (or Not?)

"All right, people," Stella called, twenty minutes later. "Let's be calm—there's no reason to push!"

When Harvey had turned on the supply closet's light, the long, terrifying nightmare had, at last, come to an end. Harvey and Stella had bustled around, leading dozens and dozens of confused, befuddled people back through the wormhole to their own dimension.

"Let's keep the line moving," Stella called. "One at a time, please. One at a— Mr. Kowalski!"

A slightly dazed-looking man in a rumpled suit and tie emerged from the wormhole, blinking up at Harvey and Stella in confusion. "What happened?" he asked, peering around the supply closet in bewilderment. "How long have I been gone?"

"Not long," Stella assured him, helping him to his feet. "Don't worry—we still have time to get the

latest issue of the *Strangeville School Gazette* to print!"

Mr. Kowalski stared blankly at her. "Gazette?" he asked. "What gazette? I'm sorry, are you one of my students?"

Stella gaped up at him in alarm.

Harvey ushered Mr. Kowalski toward the door. "Don't worry about that right now," he told the befuddled teacher. "Why don't you just go relax in the teachers' lounge for a while? Maybe get a cup of coffee?"

"Yes," Mr. Kowalski mumbled dazedly, stumbling out the door. "That sounds good. I'll just get a cup of . . . coffee. Whatever that is."

"He'll be fine," Harvey told Stella as they watched the teacher wobble away down the hallway. "I'm sure he just needs a little time. After all, it's not every day that you escape an interdimensional nightmare world."

Stella shivered.

"I can still picture the Tooth Fairy," she told Harvey, stooping to help the last person through the wormhole. "You know, for someone so obsessed with dental hygiene, its breath was *awful.*"

Harvey gave a snort of laughter as he ushered

the woman through the door, pointing her in the direction of the stairs to the front office. Finally, he and Stella were alone.

There was a moment of awkward silence.

Stella broke it first.

"Thanks," she said, tucking back a loose strand of hair. "I don't know what I would have done if you hadn't shown up."

Harvey waved her off. "I'm sure you would have thought of something," he said, blushing.

"Maybe," Stella said. "But I'm glad I didn't *have* to." Her gaze flickered to Harvey's wings, now folded behind his back. "And don't worry," she added quickly. "I'm not going to tell anyone about your wings. *Really.*"

"I know," Harvey said. He pulled her notebook out of his pocket, showing it to her. "I found the page you tore out in your notebook. You erased your notes about me."

"Yeah, well," Stella said, looking down at the floor. "I decided that maybe you were right. Sometimes I get so carried away chasing down a story that I don't even stop to think about who I might be hurting."

Harvey shook his head. "I'm sorry too," he said.

"I shouldn't have said what I said. I was just . . . hurt."

Stella held out her hand, looking up at him. "Friends?" she asked.

Harvey reached out and shook her hand. "Friends," he agreed. "And, hey, if you want to write a story about my wings, you can." He shrugged, his iridescent wings flexing behind him. "It's not like I'm going to be able to keep them a secret much longer anyway. And besides, I'm starting to think you might be right about the whole 'weird is good' thing. I mean, they *did* come in handy today," he admitted.

It was Stella's turn to shake her head. "*You* were right," she said. "It's not my secret to tell. And, besides, I have a *way* more exciting story to write now," she added, gesturing around the supply closet. "I'm thinking 'Hero Fifth Graders Save the School!' as the headline. What do you think?"

Harvey grinned. "I like it," he said. "Speaking of which, you'll probably need this back." He held Stella's notebook out to her, but to his surprise, she didn't take it.

"Why don't you keep it?" she asked.

Harvey blinked. "Seriously?"

"Every reporter worth their salt needs a note-book," Stella told him. "If you still want to help me out with the *Gazette,* that is," she added.

Harvey slid the notebook back into his pocket. "Thanks," he said simply.

The word felt strangely inadequate.

"We should take a picture," he said, pulling the camera strap off his neck. Stella grinned, coming to stand next to him. His old-fashioned film camera wasn't exactly made for selfies, but Harvey made it work as best he could.

"Say 'cheese,'" he said, holding the camera out in front of them. "One, two, three—"

"Banana!" Stella chimed in as Harvey snapped the picture.

He turned to look at her.

"What?" she asked, shrugging. "I'm lactose in-tolerant."

Harvey laughed. Looping the camera strap back around his neck, he peered thoughtfully around the small supply closet.

"You know," he told Stella. "If I'm going to be tak-ing pictures for the *Gazette,* I could probably use a darkroom. If you got rid of the shelves, this place would kind of be perfect."

"Really?" Stella asked dubiously. "You're not worried about the closet going all, you know ... *evil* again?"

"It was never really *evil*," Harvey said. "In the end, it was just ... lonely. I think maybe it would *like* the chance to be useful."

A darkroom, huh?

The supply closet's whisper was soft in his ear, a quiet echo of its once-terrifying voice.

I suppose that might be okay. For now.

Harvey rolled his eyes.

"Come on," Stella said, heading for the door. "We should get back to class."

Harvey nodded in agreement. He reached for the dangling cord, intending to turn off the light, then thought better of it.

"Maybe I'll leave the light on for a while," he told Stella, following her out the door. "Just in case."

"Just in case," Stella agreed. "After all," she said, shutting the door firmly behind him, "this *is* Strangeville."

40

An Announcement

Good afternoon, Strangeville School! And what an afternoon it has been! This is Vice Principal Capozzi, checking in with a few last-minute announcements before the final bell rings.

First off, a quick note that all students should please use caution when exiting the school today, as a giant mutant rat has left a rather . . . *unfortunate* mess in the first-floor hallway. I don't know what Cuddles has been eating, but let's just say it has *not* agreed with him.

Janitor Gary assures me that cleanup will be a breeze and that he is *more* than qualified to operate a bulldozer, despite what his license may or may *not* say.

That's the spirit, Janitor Gary! You've got to love that confidence!

Moving on, I'm pleased to announce the results of this year's science fair! In first place is Eunice Snart-waffle with her project "My Brother's Socks: Fruit or Vegetable?" Congratulations, Eunice, and enjoy your five-thousand-dollar grand prize! And another round of congratulations to our runner-up, Nevaeh Taylor, who will receive a lifetime supply of off-brand cotton swabs. "Z-Tips: Shove 'em in your ear!"

In other, *wonderful* news, I've just been informed that several dozen missing students and teachers have mysteriously reappeared on the second-floor landing, clutching boxes of office supplies and babbling incoherently to themselves. If their muddled ravings are to be believed, the supply closet has, at long last, been vanquished!

Welcome back, weary travelers! I hope you all remember your locker combinations.

And last but not least, I'm happy to report that a new lost-and-found box has been placed in the cafeteria! Although no one seems to know quite where the box came from, or why it appears to glow with a strange, eerie light of its own, I would encourage all

Strangeville students to stop by and check it out. Why, just a few minutes ago, I "found" my beloved childhood teddy bear, Mr. Buttons, whom I lost many years ago on a trip to Upper Saskatchewan!

It is *wonderful* to be reunited with Mr. Buttons, although I must say, I don't remember him having quite so many sharp, pointed teeth. . . .

Oh well.

I'm sure it's fine!

And so, Strangeville, this is Vice Principal Capozzi, signing off.

Remember, be kind. Be safe. Be curious. But most of all . . . be afraid.

Acknowledgments

I'm forever in debt to my amazing agent, Carrie Hannigan, who went above and beyond for this book. Thanks to Ellen Goff and the rest of the HG Literary team as well. I'm so grateful to be working with the wonderful Caroline Abbey, who read a messy first draft and saw the potential for so much more. Thanks to everyone at Random House for turning *Strangeville* into a real book, including April Ward and Jen Valero. A special thanks to Brett Helquist for bringing the characters to life. My kids, Wyle and Fitz, are pretty great and probably deserve to be thanked. And always last but never least, thank you to my husband, Ben, for being spectacular in every possible way. Except bowling.

About the Author

Matthew Tredinnick

DARCY MILLER is the author of *Roll, Margot and Mateo Save the World,* and *Strangeville School Is Totally Normal.* She lives in Wisconsin with her two children, her librarian husband, and way too many pets.

darcyamiller.com

About the Illustrator

Chris Lindsay

BRETT HELQUIST is the illustrator of many books, including A Series of Unfortunate Events by Lemony Snicket, *Chasing Vermeer* by Blue Balliett, *Guitar Genius* by Kim Tomsic, and *Cezanne's Parrot* by Amy Guglielmo. He is also the author of *Bedtime for Bear, Grumpy Goat,* and *Roger, the Jolly Pirate.* He grew up in Utah and now lives in Brooklyn, New York, with his wife and two kids. When he's not working, he's usually trying to play his guitar.

bretthelquist.com